HELPED BY AVA

A SWEET ROMANTIC COMEDY

REMI CARRINGTON

PRESS

❀ Created with Vellum

CHAPTER 1

AVA

*L*ife as a housekeeper and a cook didn't sound glamorous, but for the most part, I loved it. There were days when I wished I hadn't ended up still single at fifty. Spending my days taking care of rough and tumble cowboys left me exhausted when the sun went down, but this was my life. And I liked it.

I'd seen all the jokes about the odds of getting married after forty. I imagined those odds were even worse after fifty. But I'd come to believe it was based less on age and more on the person. And I wasn't born for that kind of happily ever after.

Instead, I immersed myself in life at the ranch, doing what I did best—taking care of people and feeding them.

Today, I was trying to do both things at the same time.

Relaxing by the pool wasn't possible with a five-year-old splashing in the water. I worried that if I took my eyes off him for even a second, he'd go under. "Mason, sweetie, you'll have to get out soon. Miss Ava has to check on her pies."

"Pie!" He spun in a circle, creating a giant wave.

Mason's dad was one of the ranch hands. Everyone

pitched in to look after the kid. He was a sunny addition to the ranch. Unmarried at my age, I wasn't ever going to have children of my own. And I enjoyed looking after the little guy. Especially because I could send him home to his dad at night.

"These pies are for the church. I'll bake you a pie tomorrow." I picked up the towel. "Hop out and dry off. You can stay out here but don't get back in the pool while I'm inside."

Beau walked into view. "I'll watch him." The plate in his hand soured my stomach. He'd gotten into the pies. "Oh, don't worry about dinner. I'm preheating the oven to throw in some frozen pizzas. We're having a poker night."

"Stay with Mason." I hurried inside, worried about what I'd find. The word preheating concerned me.

Pizza required a higher temp than the pies I had in the oven.

Clint sat at the counter with a slice of apple pie on his plate. "The pies were a nice surprise. They're great. But something must've dripped in the oven. Smells burnt." My brother's comment confirmed my fears.

I yanked open the oven door and waved away the smoke before pulling two black pies out of the oven. Holding back tears, I scanned the counter. All four of the pies I'd already made had at least one slice missing.

"The pies were for the church. I was supposed to drop them off in a bit." I untied my apron, picked up my purse, and walked toward the door.

"We didn't know. I'm sorry." Clint ran after me. "Ava, are you okay?"

"I'll figure it out." I fished keys out of my purse. "Be sure Mason gets a piece. I'll be back later."

Getting mad wouldn't do me any good. I hadn't told anyone the pies were for the church, and I should've known their radar would kick in.

I climbed into my truck and headed toward town. There wasn't time to make more pies. And not giving pies to the church wasn't an option. That left me with one choice, and I didn't like it.

I'd have to buy them.

I was known for my homemade pies. When people talked about me, two words that were often mentioned were pies and helpful. Not a horrible way to be thought of.

Options in Stadtburg were limited when it came to getting amazing pies. Besides, I'd never hear the end of it if someone saw me buying them. But I couldn't lie and claim store-bought pies as my own.

They probably wouldn't taste like mine anyway. If I needed doughnuts or cakes, there was a great place for that in Stadtburg, but I needed pies.

Before turning onto the road, I checked the time. If I hurried, I could make it to the one bakery in San Antonio that sold pies almost as tasty as mine. Driving like I was late, I headed into town.

My grand plan fell apart when I made it to the shop. The handwritten sign on the door made me want to cry.

Sold out. Closed for the day.

I was running out of time. The closest place that sold pies was a big warehouse store. That would have to do. Thankfully, I had a membership card.

In San Antonio I didn't worry about bumping into someone I knew. If I were shopping in Stadtburg, seeing an acquaintance was inevitable.

I loved small-town living, but there were times when anonymity was preferred. I wove my cart through the aisles to the bakery section. Then I scanned the flavors and studied the crusts to see which looked the best.

Six was what I'd promised the church. But because they were store-bought pies, I'd give them eight.

That seemed only fair.

I gathered a variety of flavors and stacked them in my cart. Then with my loaded cart, I rushed to the front and found the shortest line. Three people were in front of me.

Things were going smoothly. At this rate, I might even be early.

Waiting in line gave me time to think. If I was honest with myself, I cared less about the opinions of most of the people at church and more about the opinion of the pastor. He loved my pies. He always made his way to the food table and chatted with me when I was serving pie. I liked that.

Standing there, I could almost smell his cologne.

"Hello, Ava." The voice behind me was familiar and panic-provoking. Either my thoughts were creating auditory hallucinations, or the pastor was right behind me.

I turned, trying to block the view of my cart. "Pastor Miller."

"Why so formal?" His question made me feel called out.

Most people called him Mad Dog, and my curiosity burned to know how he'd gotten that nickname. Had he been part of a biker gang? Or maybe he'd been in the military and was known for being fierce. There were no visible tattoos that gave away the reason for the name.

Also, there was no ring on his left hand. I'd checked. Multiple times.

I overcame the temptation to ask him about it—the nickname, not the tattoos or the wedding ring. But in truth, I wondered about all three. "Sorry. Habit, I guess."

He leaned in close and looked over my shoulder. "Your donation to the church supper?"

Did he think I was planning to pass them off as my own? Having the pastor think I was a liar was worse than losing my pie reputation.

"I'm so embarrassed. I've never taken store-bought pies

to a function. But the guys at the ranch cut into the pies because they didn't know they were for the church. Which is my fault. Those guys can sniff out a pie from a mile away. And I hadn't told them not to eat them. But then one of the other men turned up the oven when I had the last of the pies cooking." Complaining to the pastor wasn't my best look.

He touched my arm which always sent my brain haywire. "Ava, it's fine. If you want, I can carry them in, and no one will know."

"But I signed up."

"Things happen. That's life." He nodded as the person in front of me moved forward.

"Thank you. Is there any way I can help you?"

"I'm a little behind setting up for this reception for Reverend Saunders. The church secretary was going to do all this shopping, but she had a family emergency. That's why I'm here. And I'm cutting it close. That part is all my fault." He nodded toward the plates and cups in his cart. "I could use help setting up. But only if you have time."

"I'm happy to help. Whatever you need." I often volunteered to help when in my heart I didn't want to, but when it came to the pastor, I wanted to help.

Not only was the man incredibly good-looking, but he had a kindness to him that I found mesmerizingly attractive. I'd never admit to anyone that I enjoyed his attention, but I did. And if helping earned me a little time with him, I was happy to do it.

"Great. And I'll pay for those pies. That way when someone asks about them, I can honestly say I bought them at the warehouse store."

"You're a saint."

"I try." He winked.

I'd never met a pastor who winked before, and I wasn't

sure how to react, so I went with flaming cheeks and awkward silence.

"How is everyone out at the ranch?" Pastor Mad Dog was great at salvaging conversations.

"Good. We're all good. Clint and Joji are settling into married life. Beau and Lilith keep talking about going on a delayed honeymoon, but the venue keeps her busy. Things are good." I silently berated myself. One good was plenty, but no, I had to work three into my answer.

He inched forward when I moved up. "How are you?"

I stopped myself before responding with another 'good.' "I can't complain." And now I'd just lied to the pastor. I was more than capable of complaining, and I'd been complaining to him moments ago. This was why I stuck to conversations about pie.

But we'd already discussed the pie debacle.

"The weather is beautiful today." Weather was always a safe topic. If I'd learned anything growing up in Texas, it was that.

He nodded, and his soft brown eyes made my heart palpitate. "Very beautiful."

My heartbeat sent blood pulsing against my eardrums, and I stared at the man. We'd covered the two safe topics I depended on, and staring at him wasn't making the silence any less uncomfortable.

"Next." The cashier came to my rescue.

After Mad Dog paid for everything, he moved the pies to his cart. "I guess I'll meet you at the church."

"Yes. Do you need help loading?" I stayed beside him as we walked across the parking lot.

A man with muscular arms like his didn't require my help loading, but I always offered to help. It was a habit I wasn't sure I'd ever break. Did I need to? Helping people was a good thing.

"I'd love your help." He looked at the stack of pies. "What's the best way to get these to the church without destroying them during the drive? Would you want to ride with me? I can drive you back to get your truck afterward."

The thought of a half hour in the car with Mad Dog terrified me. What would we talk about? The bigger worry was what I would say. When I was nervous, I either talked about pies or I rambled, and sometimes that included saying nonsensical and stupid things. My words bypassed my normal filter, which was never a good thing.

I'd made it this long without embarrassing myself. Risking a car ride was out of the question. I couldn't make myself tell him no, but I could offer a helpful alternative. "When I deliver pies, I sit them in boxes on the floorboard. I have some boxes in the truck. Want me to grab them?"

"Sure." He seemed almost disappointed with my answer.

I hated disappointing people. "Actually, I will ride with you. Let me lock up my truck."

He smiled. "Thank you for all your help."

"Anytime. I'm always happy to help." I walked to my truck before I volunteered to do the man's laundry. Hopefully, I wouldn't offer anything like that on the drive to the church.

Why did I get so flustered around him? He definitely qualified as what many women called a silver fox. And when he wasn't praying, he was probably working out. The muscles hidden under his shirt gave that away. Not that I'd seen under his shirt.

Thinking about his arms wasn't going to make the drive easier. I fanned myself and locked my truck.

Breathing exercises for the next thirty minutes would hopefully get me to the church without embarrassing myself. Unless he noticed what I was doing. Maybe breathing exercises were a bad idea.

CHAPTER 2

MAD DOG

I'd eaten more pie in my attempts to spend time with Ava than I cared to admit. Anytime I hinted at the idea of spending time together, she panicked. Fear swirled in her eyes, and her muscles tensed. That was a tad hard on my ego.

She was the first woman who'd captured my attention in a long time. But beyond talking about pies and the weather, she wanted nothing to do with me. So, I spent a considerable amount of time talking about pies and weather.

Her decision to ride with me came as a surprise. A nice surprise.

And when I spotted her fanning herself as she walked to her truck, a glimmer of hope flickered. By Texas standards, the temperatures were mild, so I guessed she wasn't hot. Maybe I'd misread her reaction.

Not long after we pulled out of the parking lot, it was obvious that if we were going to talk, I would have to start the conversation. "How long have you worked at the ranch?"

"About thirty years." She shifted the stack of pies in her lap.

"A long time. Did you start working there when you were in high school?"

She didn't seem older than maybe forty-five, if even that old.

Her laugh made me question that assumption.

"Funny. No. I wasn't in high school." She chewed her bottom lip. "How is your daughter? She's in New York, right?"

Ava had remembered. And she was talking about something other than pie. I'd be happy if this trend continued.

"Poppy seems to enjoy living there. I miss her, but if she's happy, I'm happy." I'd only mentioned my daughter once when Ava and I had discussed apple pie. That was Poppy's favorite.

Ava stared at the stack in her lap. "I am sorry about the pies."

"I'm sure these don't taste as good as yours, but people will eat them just the same. Don't worry about it."

"I'll try. I mean try to not . . ." She shook her head. "You know what I mean."

"Once the reception is over, I won't linger. I don't want to keep you too late."

"If you need to stay, I can find someone to drive me back to my truck."

"No need for that. I'm happy to do it." I was hoping we could expand our list of conversation topics on the ride back to her truck. When we arrived at church, I parked in my reserved spot. "I'll run around and get those pies."

Not only did she have four stacked in her lap, but there were four boxes sitting on the floorboard between her feet. When I leaned in to pick up the boxes, she sucked in a breath.

Did I make her nervous?

"Slide those other boxes on top of these." Surely, I could carry the pies into the building without dropping them.

"Are you sure?" Ava didn't have faith in me.

"Yep. Pile them on."

She did, and my ability to see where I was headed disappeared.

"You'll have to steer me." I chuckled, aware that it was a tad awkward to ask her to do that.

With her hand on my wrist, she said, "All right. Take two steps forward." She continued giving instructions, and I followed them.

When we made it to the door, Ava's hand slipped off my wrist. "Let me get the door."

Nothing happened.

"Um, it's locked."

"The other volunteers must not have arrived yet here yet. The keys are . . ." They were in my pocket. I could turn around and try to make it to the truck to set the pies down to grab my keys, or I could ask Ava to reach into my pocket.

"They're in your pocket. I can see the top of the keychain sticking out."

"Would you mind?"

"I'm definitely getting to know you better today." She gave a nervous laugh. "What's your favorite pie flavor?"

"If I start talking about pie, I'll drop all of them." I waited for the squeak of the door.

Her fingers touched my wrist. "It's open. Are we going into the fellowship hall?"

"That'd be great."

She guided me down the hall and nudged me when I needed to turn. "The tables are all set up. Put the stack here."

I walked until I bumped into a table, then set all eight pies down undamaged.

"I'm going to get the room set up while we're waiting for the other ladies." She lifted boxes off the stack and sorted the pies by flavor.

I rubbed her shoulder. "Thank you so much."

She glanced at my hand, then smiled.

Ava knew where everything was. It wasn't the first time she'd helped out at the church. And in a short time, she had all the serving tables draped with tablecloths. "The other ladies will set out the food. But the tables are ready. How else can I help?"

"Someone dropped off a huge batch of lemon bars this morning. They are sitting on my desk. Would you mind grabbing them?" I shifted the ladder, ready to put in the second nail to hang the Welcome sign.

"Sure, but please be careful on that ladder." With an authority rarely seen from her, she pointed at me. "Don't fall."

"Yes, ma'am." I hadn't seen that side of Ava, and I liked it. A lot. As I reached up to hammer in the second nail, I dropped the dang thing. And I couldn't find it on the floor. I was nearly convinced they became invisible once they hit the floor. Thankfully, I had more nails in my office.

Remembering that Ava was getting the lemon bars, I pushed open the door carefully.

She smiled. "You weren't joking. Someone spent a lot of time making this many lemon bars."

That smile flashed in my mind often when she wasn't anywhere near me. Maybe now was a good time to tell her that.

"Mad Dog!"

Her panicked yell ripped me out of my thoughts. She was falling.

I lunged toward her, hoping to stop her fall. Saving Ava and the lemon bars didn't seem possible. But catching her was my priority.

And I succeeded.

With half of the gooey desserts smashed between us and

the rest raining down on my rug, I wrapped my arms around her. "Whoa."

"Oh my." She inhaled and met my gaze. "Thank you."

Nothing in me wanted to let go. But feeling her body tense, I loosened my embrace and shifted. My foot landed on a lemon bar, and gravity took over.

We were falling again. This time, together.

Ava landed on top of me, and I instinctively wrapped my arms around her again.

"I'm so sorry." Horror filled her big brown eyes.

She had nothing to apologize for. Besides the lemon goo everywhere, there was nothing unpleasant about our current arrangement. At least in my opinion.

I brushed a smudge of lemon off her cheek, then licked my finger. "Tasty."

My comment had the desired effect, and her body relaxed against mine. "It looks good." She dabbed her finger in a glob on my cheek and tasted a bite. "These *are* good. I might have to get the recipe."

"Ava, maybe when this is over—"

She bit into her bottom lip. "Oh no. The reception. You're a complete mess thanks to me." Still on top of me, she wiped my shirt, which was a wasted effort. "I really am sorry. I must've tripped on air. Which takes talent, I know. But that's me. Talented."

"It was probably this stupid rug. The edges curl no matter what I do." Kissing the lemon filling off her face was tempting but probably ill advised.

Her eyes widened and she pushed on my chest, her hands sliding as she did. "I'm probably crushing you."

I pulled her closer, not wanting to waste the moment. "Ava—"

She went pale and stopped moving. Her gaze wasn't focused on me, but on the doorway.

I tipped my head back to see who'd shown up at just the right moment. "Reverend Saunders. You're early."

Lying on the floor with Ava on top of me and lemon smeared everywhere was not what the man needed to see. Hopefully, he wasn't the gossiping type.

"It seems I came at an inconvenient time." He adjusted his glasses. "You're married?"

"Not yet." Ava giggled in a strange way. "I was just helping him, you know, get ready. With the pies."

Ava wasn't helping.

And why did Reverend Saunders jump to that conclusion? Where did it say that being married was a prerequisite to rolling around in smashed lemon bars? That question didn't need to be asked right now. Or ever.

He walked out of the office and closed the door without saying another word. I held back a groan. While there was wiggle room in what Ava had said, I knew he'd left thinking that Ava and I were going to be married.

I had so much explaining to do.

Ava sniffled, and all thoughts of the minister were obliterated by the tears brimming in her eyes.

"I'm so sorry. I didn't mean to say that. When I'm nervous, words just roll out. Normally, I just talk about pie." She blinked, but it only caused the tears to spill out and slip down her cheeks.

I tried wiping a tear away and ended up spreading lemon filling and cookie crumbs across her face. "Please don't cry. It's fine. I'll talk to him."

"He'll either think I'm nuts or a liar." She pushed on my chest, then rolled off me.

I scrambled to my feet, avoiding the slick spots. "Careful getting up." I held out my hand to her.

Gripping my hand, she managed to get on her feet but skidded on the slippery filling.

I caught her around the waist. "Whoa. We don't want to end up on the floor again."

There was a small part of me that maybe wanted to end up on the floor again, but with volunteers showing up soon and the reverend around, that wasn't the wisest choice.

She leaned her head on my shoulder. "I won't be at church for a while. Maybe a year."

My heart sank, and I pulled her closer. "Don't say that. This isn't a big deal. Really."

The door opened, and I decided that I needed to install a voice-activated lock. Did they even make those?

Mrs. Beecham gasped. "My lemon bars!"

Ava shoved away from me and darted toward the door. Mrs. Beecham jumped out of the way faster than I'd ever seen her move.

"Sorry about the lemon bars. We had a bit of an accident." I dragged my fingers through my hair and instantly regretted it.

"An accident? Really?" She huffed as she stormed away.

There would definitely be gossip.

As much as I wanted to chase Ava, I had problems that needed attention. I kicked off my shoes at the door, hoping not to leave a lemony trail everywhere I went.

Where was Ava going anyway? I was her ride. Handling problems would have to wait. I ran down the hall to find her, then spotted the door to the ladies' room closing.

Not thinking clearly, I burst into the bathroom. "Ava?"

The yelp from the stall didn't sound anything like Ava.

"Sorry." I was making things worse.

As I trudged back down the hall, I noticed light peeking out from the janitor's closet. Barging in hadn't worked so well, so this time I knocked.

The door opened a sliver. "I'll be in here until it's over."

Ava didn't stick her head out far enough for me to see her face.

The door closed.

"Ava, wait."

The door didn't open again. And I couldn't blame her.

Helping me had left her stranded in the janitor's closet and covered in sweet goo.

Frustrated with the whole situation, I went in search of Reverend Saunders.

Because he was from the district office, I needed to clear up the situation. Even though he was about to retire, he still had connections, and I didn't want wrong assumptions being passed on.

Reverend Saunders was in the kitchen, sampling pies. The twinkle in his eye relaxed me a little. Pointing at me with his fork, he said, "Even at your age, you shouldn't wait too long to get married. I'd be honored to perform the ceremony."

My heart landed in my stomach. He'd made huge assumptions.

"We, um . . . she tripped. Then I tripped. We aren't—" I couldn't for the life of me get out a complete sentence.

He reached out to pat my arm but stopped before touching me. "It's good she's your fiancée. Being in such a compromising position with a congregant would be scandalous."

Was he joking with me?

"Scandalous is right!" Mrs. Beecham sucked all the air out of the room. "And they ruined my lemon bars."

Mrs. Beecham was the type of woman who could whip up a scandal out of nothing at all. Asking for the lemon bar recipe in hopes of distracting her probably wouldn't work.

Reverend Saunders shook his head. "It's okay. They'll be married soon. No reason to panic."

He was serious. How had slipping on lemon bars escalated to scandal so quickly?

I needed to set the record straight. "Sir, we aren't—"

Mrs. Beecham scrunched up her face. "To *Ava*?" She spat out the name as if it tasted bad.

The condemnation in her question inflamed my temper.

"Why not Ava?" This was not handling it, but my mouth had a mind of its own. My retort only fueled the idea that Ava and I were together.

The woman had the nerve to act wounded by my question. "In my day we'd have called her an *old maid*, and she's *fat*." Mrs. Beecham emphasized the last word, raising her voice a little.

She was easily two decades older than me, but that was no excuse for being impolite. I nearly said that last part out loud. And I considered calling her old.

But I didn't.

With a deep breath I tempered my rage and tried to figure out what I could say that would be constructive. Something more appropriate for the pastor to say.

The truth seemed the best choice. "I think she's beautiful."

Mrs. Beecham's hand flew to her chest, and if drama weren't part of everything she did, I'd worry she was having a heart issue.

The minister intervened before she choked out any words. "Would you like some pie? It's very good. Tastes almost homemade."

My knot of emotions exploded as laughter, and I walked out of the room. "I need to change clothes."

Thankfully, I always kept a clean suit in my office. I'd be overdressed for the reception, but I wouldn't be smeared with lemon.

Sadly, I didn't have anything to offer Ava, but how would

that look if I had her clothes in my office? Or if she showed up to the reception wearing something of mine?

When I made it to my office, I shut the door, steered clear of the mess on the rug in front of my desk, and then closed myself into the private bathroom. Getting the lemon off my face and out of my hair was required before I even attempted to put on clean clothes.

CHAPTER 3

AVA

*A*s much as I wanted to run away and never again return to the church, leaving Mad Dog with that mess would consume me with guilt. I'd clean up, and then I'd run away.

Thankful for the sink in the closet, I unrolled a wad of paper towels and turned on the shop sink. Heat rippled through every muscle at the memory of Mad Dog's arms around me. When we were so close, I worried he could read my thoughts. Because when he was close, my heart pounded in unnatural ways.

Thinking about it was making me feverish. That wasn't a good look.

After cleaning the lemon filling off me as best I could, I rummaged through the janitor's closet until I found a bucket and a brush. The only soap I found was lemon scented. Even the cleaning supplies were laughing at me.

Oddly, I couldn't find trash bags. This seemed like a good place to keep them. But I knew where I could get some.

I poked my head out of the bathroom. Bumping into

someone sounded about as appealing as eating Beau's cooking. Not recommended . . . unless it came off the grill.

Even if whoever it was hadn't heard about what happened, they'd ask why my clothes were wet. Not a conversation I wanted to have.

Today had been a series of unfortunate happenings, but if there was one thing I could do right, it was clean.

Poor Mad Dog was probably still trying to explain the scene to the minister. As for Mrs. Beecham, it was best for me not to think about her. She made me want to say things inappropriate for church.

After scanning the hall to be sure it was empty, I carried the bucket into Mad Dog's office and dropped to my knees. With a lot of work and a little luck, I could have the rug cleaned up before the reception was over.

I needed something to clean up the chunks before I could tackle what had gotten rubbed into the rug. The closet in the kitchen had a stash of rags and trash bags. Both of those would come in handy.

I walked partway down the hall, then after sneaking in through the side door of the kitchen, I peeked through the open serving window. Mrs. Beecham and Reverend Saunders were standing near the tables. If I stayed low, they wouldn't see me. I ducked as I walked past the counter. Having to talk to either of them would only make this day worse.

In the closet, the rags were right where they were supposed to be, and I grabbed a handful. Then I silently tugged two trash bags out of the box.

Crouching in the doorway, I checked again before crossing the kitchen but stopped when my name was mentioned.

"Are you sure he isn't marrying Ava?" Reverend Saunders sounded so somber.

"*Marrying Ava?* You can't be serious. Of course he's not. What she was doing was scandalous." Mrs. Beecham's shrill voice made me want to smack her.

I also hated that she was right. Of course Mad Dog wasn't marrying me. The thought was ridiculous.

"Hmmm." Reverend Saunders dragged out the sound. "If he's not marrying her, that's a bit concerning."

"Such a scandal. We need to convene a meeting. It's a good thing you're here." Mrs. Beecham was probably lighting a torch and getting ready to gather a mob.

Where was Mad Dog? Did he know about this?

I'd ruined the man's job.

Without sticking around to hear Mrs. Beecham drag Mad Dog through the mud, I hurried back to the office and wedged a chair against the door. Alone, I could clean and cry. What had started out as a bad day had progressively gotten worse. The safest thing was for me to be alone. I couldn't hurt anyone that way.

The thought of riding back to get my truck with Mad Dog knotted my insides. Not only was I sticky and gross, but I would also spend the entire ride feeling guilty that I'd lost him his job.

But he probably didn't even know. And I'd feel even guiltier that I wasn't telling him.

In turmoil, I scraped lemon goo off the rug, then shoved rags in the trash. I could buy the church new rags. I needed to do that soon, or Mrs. Beecham would tell everyone that I'd stolen the rags.

She meant well.

After using several rags to wipe up as much as I could, I started the hard part. Scrubbing.

The dessert combined with the cleaner guaranteed this office would smell like lemons for weeks. Maybe longer.

As I dragged the scrub brush back and forth, I berated

myself for what I'd said. *Not yet.* My tears mixed with the sudsy water. Salt water was probably horrible for the rug, but that couldn't be helped.

What I hadn't told Mad Dog was that I got nervous around him. Being around him made my brain hum, and rational thought often went to lunch when I needed it most. But none of that mattered now.

Was there any way to save Mad Dog's job? I replayed what the minister had said. *If he isn't marrying Ava . . .*

It seemed like there was only one way to fix things. Poor Mad Dog. What a horrible choice—marry Ava or lose his job.

A door opened, and I looked toward the chair. It was still wedged in place. I turned back around just in time to see Mad Dog race back into the bathroom in his boxer briefs.

Surely this was as bad as the day could get.

The bathroom door opened a crack. "Um, Ava?"

I covered my eyes. "I'm sorry." How many times had I apologized today? Was there a world record for that? If there was, I was probably vying for the title. "I didn't know you were in here."

"I was thinking the same thing. I didn't mean to . . . well, you know." He cleared his throat. "Could you hand me the suit hanging on the inside of the closet door?"

"Of course." Careful not to get lemon on his clothes and making sure I never actually looked at the door, I held out the suit. "I'm so sorry."

The door closed, and laughter echoed in the bathroom. "Don't worry about it. We'll chat once I'm dressed."

I went back to scrubbing. My efforts were gleaning little reward. Sticky lemon was caked into the fibers. I might have to buy the man a new rug. But I wasn't done trying to save this one. If I could save this rug, maybe Mad Dog wouldn't lose his job. The parallel made no sense, but that didn't stop me from scrubbing.

Mad Dog walked out of the bathroom dressed in slacks and a dress shirt, and he looked good. Really good. "Please stop cleaning. *Please.*"

"I was just trying to—"

"I'm going to throw out the rug. I should've thrown it out weeks ago. I'm sorry you tripped."

"I'm okay." That was more than I could say for Mad Dog's job. Using the edge of the desk to get up, I tried to avoid looking like a panda rolling around. There was no easy way to tell him what I'd heard. And I wasn't ready to talk about it anyway. My thoughts were too scattered. Pointing at the door, I picked up the bucket. "I should go."

"I'm so sorry, Ava. I can . . ." He ran his fingers through his wet hair. "Your truck is in San Antonio. If you don't mind waiting for a little while, I can cut this reception short or possibly just slip out early."

"I've messed everything up. I really am sorry." How many apologies were appropriate when you blundered a man out of a job?

He stepped closer, and I backed away.

"Ava, don't worry about it. I'm sure it won't be a problem. By tomorrow people will have forgotten all about it."

If by people he meant me, then it wasn't true. I'd be thinking about this for a long time to come. The worst of it was, I'd never felt more comfortable with Mad Dog than when we were laughing about being smeared in lemon. Aside from worrying that I was crushing the poor man.

But I'd never been more horrified than when Reverend Saunders showed up.

I moved further away from Mad Dog. "I'll just stay in here."

He moved the chair away from the knob. "You can put this back if you want. I'll knock."

"Thanks."

Once he was out the door, I yanked out my phone and sent a text to my friends Lilith and Joji. I didn't want Beau or Clint finding out about the disaster with the pastor, but Lilith and Joji were my closest friends. I could beg them to keep a secret or simply not tell them why I reeked of lemon. The second option sounded better.

HELP. I need a ride from the church back to the ranch and then to San Antonio to pick up my truck. Either of you available? After hitting send, I stared at the phone.

On my way! Joji answered within seconds.

Having those two ladies on the ranch had made my life fuller.

A quick glance left and right assured me that Mrs. Beecham wasn't waiting to pounce. I slipped out the back door and waited in the shadows.

Was it fair to blame Beau and Clint for my bad day? Thanks to them, I'd given store-bought pies to the church, been caught tangled up with the pastor, and had seen him in only his underwear.

Any one of those was awful. That last part wasn't so horrible, but I wouldn't admit that to anyone.

The three combined made me want to move to Australia.

Joji pulled into the lot, and after lining the seat with a trash bag, I climbed inside.

"Quick. Drive." I didn't want Mad Dog to run out and see that I was leaving. Scrolling through my phone, I prayed I still had his number. Months ago, he'd messaged me details about an event. If I could find his number, then he wouldn't end the reception early on my account.

I finally found the number and sent him a text: *Found a ride.* I typed out *I'm sorry*, then deleted it. I'd used those words too many times.

What if Mad Dog was right? Maybe by tomorrow, no one would be talking about what happened with the lemon bars.

No part of me believed that.

Joji remained silent until we turned onto the road by the ranch. "What happened? You smell like lemon pie, and you look like you've been rolling in it."

How could she see that in the dark cab? The fact that I'd lined the seat was probably a clue.

"I had an accident with a huge batch of lemon bars." I conveniently left out the part about Mad Dog being a part of that accident. "I know it's inconvenient, but I want to clean up before running into town to get my truck. Is that okay?"

Poor Mad Dog had to stay at church. If he got wind of the meeting Mrs. Beecham wanted to convene, he probably wouldn't speak to me ever again. I wouldn't blame him.

Why had I opened my big mouth? Why had I offered to help him set up for the reception? I knew the answer. Helping him meant being around him, and I liked being near Mad Dog. Too much.

Joji pulled through the ranch gate. "No problem. After we pick up your truck, we can watch a movie. The guys are playing poker tonight, so company would be nice."

"I'm not sure about a movie."

"Come on. Even after running into town, it will still be early. Way too early for bed on a Saturday night. And I bet Lilith will join us after her event finishes." Joji tapped the steering wheel. "It'll be fun."

"All right." A funny movie and a glass of wine would be a good distraction.

Joji POURED two glasses then cued up a movie. "The Proposal okay? I love Sandra Bullock, and I don't think I've seen this one."

"Fine with me. I'm not sure I've seen that one either." I

snuggled into one end of the sofa and checked my phone when it buzzed.

I stifled a groan when I read Mad Dog's text. *I'll see you tomorrow.*

He wouldn't. Not at church anyway. I wasn't planning to go back there for several weeks. Maybe months. Maybe never.

Sipping my wine, I watched the movie plot unfold, and panic multiplied in my chest. Watching a story about two people who were getting married just to save her job was not going to help me forget my blunder . . . or that Mad Dog was going to get booted from his job.

When one of the characters walked out of the bathroom in a towel and ended up on the floor with his boss, I nearly covered my eyes. This was the wrong movie to watch if I wanted to forget any part of what had happened today.

My imagination took over, and I pictured Mad Dog standing at the front of the sanctuary while the biddies flung lemons at him. And all the while, I stood in the back of the room, watching and not doing anything to stop it.

Watching the romantic comedy made me feel guilty. Should I offer to marry Mad Dog so he could keep his job? Unlike the movie, my offer of help wouldn't lead to love. Long ago, I gave up hoping for that sort of happy ending.

But if I could help Mad Dog, maybe I should.

I'd sleep on it and make a decision in the morning.

SLEEPING on it sounded like a great idea except I couldn't sleep. My brain wouldn't let me. The scene with the flying lemons played over and over in my head. Finally, well after three in the morning, the scene changed. I raced to the front and grabbed Mad Dog's hand.

When I did, the ladies quieted, probably too shocked to talk. But no one threw any more fruit at Mad Dog.

The infuriating part of the dream was that once I walked out of the shadows, I could no longer see Mad Dog's face.

His reaction to my bold move was completely obscured. The idea of marrying me would probably horrify him. It was like offering him old, nearly rotten food. But the kind thing to do—the helpful thing—would be to offer.

CHAPTER 4

MAD DOG

*A*ll night I'd replayed the episode in my head over and over. Why couldn't Reverend Saunders have waited ten more minutes? Five even. I'd finally worked up the nerve and was going to ask Ava out. That hadn't gone as planned.

Then she'd left without even a goodbye.

I hoped that the whole thing had died down and that I wouldn't hear a word about it at church today.

Every Sunday, volunteers laid out pastries in the fellowship hall. And I needed a little something to go with my fourth cup of coffee. The looks on their faces disintegrated my hope that yesterday's event had been forgotten. The story was spreading.

I blamed Mrs. Beecham. Reverend Saunders didn't seem quite the type for gossip, but I didn't know the man that well.

While the ladies set out food and put centerpieces on tables, I carried my doughnut into the hall, watching for Ava. Would she show up today? I had my doubts.

I stepped into the kitchen, headed back to get another doughnut, and heard someone mention Ava. With my back against the wall, I listened to the discussion in the fellowship hall.

"How embarrassing for Ava to throw herself at him like that. She could have at least destroyed her own pies."

"Ava is a sweet person. I believe it was an accident." One kind voice stood out among the vipers.

"Seriously? They were on the floor and *then* hugging standing up. So I'm not buying the accident story. But poor Ava. Does she really think the pastor would want her?"

In my fury, my ability to distinguish voices was absent. Probably for the best. Putting faces to the ugly words they were saying wouldn't help me be polite when I interacted with them.

"I heard she was on *top* of him. It's lucky she didn't break him."

I'd had about all I could take.

"What I want to know is if she's doing that with him, who else is she carrying on with? Because it seems to me like she's trying to nab a husband." Mrs. Beecham's tone was accusatory and condescending. "Some women will go to any lengths to get a man. There are other ladies around here—younger and prettier—for the pastor to date. She should know that."

The hateful, hurtful words these women passed around at church made me angry. Had Ava ever heard them talking about her? Was that why she was so horrified by the whole incident?

I had to remind myself that not everyone was being rude. Only a handful of people had said anything, and one even jumped to Ava's defense. But the awful words bounced around in my head.

How many times had I told couples that love was a decision? These ladies made relationships sound trite. And somehow their biting words gave me the courage to do what

I'd wanted to do for months. What I'd almost done yesterday. I'd ask Ava out. It was time for me to stop acting like a chicken.

If she'd overheard people talking about her, maybe that was why she steered conversations toward pie and weather. I'd always given up when she did. But if she'd ever heard anything remotely like this, I couldn't blame her.

"What else can you expect from Ava? She lives out there on the ranch with all those guys." Another faceless person piled on.

I needed to break up this little gossip party. Smiling, I strolled into the fellowship hall. "Hello, ladies."

They all fell silent. Watching their faces go pale amused me. Maybe I'd title my next sermon 'If you can't say it in front of the pastor, maybe you shouldn't say it at all.'

The volunteers stood around quietly while I chose a second pastry. Preaching on gossip this morning would be too obvious.

But I was tempted.

AFTER CHURCH I drove out to Ava's. It bothered me that she hadn't come to church. Maybe asking her out today wasn't a great idea. I'd talked myself out of it so many times, but I didn't want her to feel pressured.

After being married and then widowed, I'd been out of the dating game too long. Every time I saw Ava, I sought her out. But I'd talked myself out of asking her out even though I really wanted to get to know her better. And look where it had gotten me.

At the ranch I pulled up to the main house. Ava lived on the ranch somewhere, but I didn't know where, so I'd have to start here.

I knocked, and Beau yanked open the door.

"Hiya, minister. What can I do for you?" He stepped back and motioned for me to enter. "I didn't know there was an event today. Need me to grab Lilith? I keep telling her she needs to hire someone to help with the venue. That place is busy."

"I'm not here for an event. I was looking for Ava." Choosing my words carefully would save Ava and me lots of embarrassment.

Beau grinned. "She played hooky from church this morning, and you are here to get after her, huh?"

"No. Not at all. Nothing like that." Was that what people thought of me? I stepped back as a large cat raced by.

Beau chuckled. "Don't mind Princess. She won't hurt you. At least I don't think."

I didn't want to test that. "Is Ava around?"

"Haven't seen her in a while. Have you checked her house?"

"Point me in the right direction, and I'll head over there." I hoped I'd find her in a place where we could talk privately.

Beau stepped out the front door. "Go back the way you came and veer a left at the fork. Continue uphill past the three cabins on the right, then past the house on the left. Ava's house is the next one. Her truck will be in the driveway if she's home."

"Thanks." I rushed out before he could ask any other questions.

I followed his directions and was relieved to see Ava's truck parked where he said it would be. Silently rehearsing what I wanted to say, I knocked on the door.

Ava opened the door, and her eyes went wide. "Pastor."

"I hope you don't mind that I stopped by. When I didn't see you at church this morning, I was concerned that you were serious about not attending for a year."

She didn't smile, which concerned me. "Haven't decided yet." Pulling the door open, she stepped aside. "Want to come in? I need to talk to you about something."

I wasn't sure what conversation was coming. But those words never heeded good news. "Is everything okay?"

She crossed her arms and inhaled. "Last night when I grabbed rags out of the kitchen, I overheard Reverend Saunders telling Mrs. Beecham that if you aren't marrying me they'll convene a meeting because of the scandal. I feel awful. I may have lost you your job."

"Don't worry about it. Really. I'm sure it's nothing." The comment about convening a meeting mildly concerned me. I hadn't heard that rumor. "I'll talk to him and see if I can make him understand that it was an accident."

"But that doesn't explain what I said. He'll think I'm a liar. But if he needs to think I tell fibs in order for you to keep your job, I can live with that. There are other churches." She wandered into the kitchen.

I followed. "I don't want you to find another church. In fact, I was hoping—"

She poured two glasses of tea. "I can only think of one way to save your job, and I'm willing to help you. He said that they will have the meeting if you *weren't* going to marry me. So, if it means not having you thrown out as pastor, I'm willing to marry you. If it will help. It's the least I can do." Staring into her glass she swallowed.

Had she just offered to marry me? I sipped my tea, trying to decide how to answer. The conversations I'd overheard thumped on my skull.

"Oh, gosh. That sounds so unbelievable. Of course you don't want to marry me. I can help you pack boxes if you end up needing to move. I wish there was something I could do. I think Mrs. Beecham has him all stirred up. She's really not a very nice lady." Ava slapped a hand over her mouth. "Sorry. I shouldn't speak ill of people."

"You'd marry me?" I kept thinking about how love was a decision.

She nodded but didn't look me in the eye. "How long will Reverend Saunders be in town?"

Maybe it was only a temporary offer. I set my glass on the counter. "He moved back here because he's about to retire. He used to pastor this church before I arrived, and he is here in a support capacity until his retirement is finalized." I set my glass down beside hers. "If we did get married, it wouldn't be a short-term thing."

She met my gaze, and there was a hint of fear in her brown eyes. "Okay."

I didn't want her to feel forced into anything. "But, Ava, I don't want to—"

"It's okay. I shouldn't have said anything. We barely know each other, and I'm not exactly your type. It makes sense that you don't want to get married." She bit her lip.

"That wasn't what I was going to say, but how about this? Sleep on it. We'll meet tomorrow and talk." I needed time to decide, and I wanted to be sure she had plenty of time to think about her choice. "This isn't a decision to be made lightly."

Ava motioned toward the table. "Do you want to eat? I can make something."

"I'll take a raincheck on that. We both need time to think." I did. I hadn't asked her out, but now I was considering asking her to marry me. I was doing everything backward.

~

I'D SPENT the rest of Sunday deciding what to do. The idea of marrying Ava—or at least proposing even if she didn't accept —felt right.

Reverend Saunders wanted to have lunch tomorrow, and I could guess the topic. Hopefully, by then, I'd have an answer from Ava. One way or the other.

Before calling Ava to schedule a time to talk, I called my daughter. If I was planning a big life change, it seemed only fair to mention it to her.

Sitting on my sofa, I dialed. It rang four times before she picked up.

"Hi, Dad."

"Hello, sweetheart. How are you?"

"Pretty much the same as I was earlier today when we chatted. What's up?" Even though we lived far apart, she could read me well.

"I'm thinking about remarrying." I held my breath, wondering how Poppy would react.

Sniffles sounded on her end of the line. "After ten years, I wasn't sure I'd ever hear you say that. Who is she?"

"A woman from church. I haven't asked yet, but if she says yes, we'll probably get married soon, and I'd love for you to be here."

"As if there is any question about whether I'd come. Of course I'll be there. Tell me about her."

"She's kind and selfless. And beautiful. I can't wait for you to meet her."

"I'm happy for you, Dad. I'd love to talk longer, but my roommate is feverishly waving her arms which means I need to go. Love you."

"Be safe." I missed having Poppy close, but she seemed to enjoy living in New York.

"Always, Dad. Bye."

I slid the phone into my pocket, then pulled it right back out and dialed Ava's number.

"Hello." The waver in her voice made me think she knew who'd called, and that made her all the more endearing.

"Ava, it's me. Mad Dog. I was calling about tomorrow. Are you free to meet for breakfast?"

"Yes, I can. But not until after nine. I serve the men breakfast at seven, then it takes a bit of time to clean up. But after that, I can meet, or I can make you breakfast."

"Would it work if I picked you up at nine thirty?"

"Yes. I'll be ready."

"Good. And, Ava, I'm really looking forward to it."

A second of silence preceded a whispered "Me too."

Before climbing into bed that night, I set an early alarm. Finding a ring before nine in the morning wasn't likely, but that wouldn't stop me from trying.

CHAPTER 5

AVA

*S*tanding in my closet, I scanned my clothes. What should I wear to breakfast? Why did he want to meet to talk about it? Couldn't he have politely told me no over the phone instead of letting me . . . hope?

The thought surprised me, but it was true. There was a tiny part of me that wanted him to take me up on the offer. I had no delusions of the marriage being like what Lilith or Joji had, but it would be a step above the life I had now. At least that was how I felt.

Entertaining the idea of a yes brought on hot flashes. More likely, he'd decline with heaps of sweet words. I couldn't bear to live through that in a restaurant.

With my thoughts in chaos, I resorted to what I knew best. In the kitchen I pulled out the ingredients for my favorite indulgent recipe, crème brûlée French toast.

By the time I had the dish in the fridge ready to slide into the oven in the morning, it was late. But I sent Mad Dog a text. *If possible, I'd like to have our conversation in private. Would it be okay if we had breakfast at my house?*

I didn't expect an answer tonight. Neither did I expect to sleep.

But only a few minutes later, my phone dinged.

Mad Dog texted: *Of course. What can I bring?*

Nothing. I didn't want him going to any trouble. I'd caused enough of that already.

In the dark, I stared at the ceiling for hours, replaying the lemon bars incident over and over in my head. Eventually, remembering how it felt to have his arms wrapped around me, I fell asleep.

In my dream, churchgoers snickered as I walked by, and lemons were being passed around the pews.

It didn't make sense. The church didn't even have pews, just rows of chairs. But the way the dream made me feel made perfect sense. How could I ever go back? It was just as well that Mad Dog would be turning down my offer. Being married to the pastor and not going to church would create a whole other set of issues.

I DOWNED two cups of coffee before the ranch hands' breakfast was anywhere close to ready. The meal itself was a blur.

As soon as the guys left the table, I hurriedly cleaned up. The French toast needed time in the oven, and Mad Dog would be at my house in just over an hour.

"Ava." Joji waved her hand in front of my face.

"When did you come back in?"

"Just now, but you seemed a million miles away. Is everything okay?" She picked up a rag and wiped down the table.

"I didn't sleep well last night. I'm in a haze." I hadn't lied, but I also had no intention of telling her the whole truth. Telling Joji meant my brother would find out that I'd volunteered to marry a guy to help him out. I didn't need a lecture.

Her eyes narrowed. "Need me to cover lunch? I don't mind."

"No. I should be fine. But if something changes, I'll let you know." I picked up my purse. "I need to run home, but I'll talk to you later."

She nodded.

When I made it back to the house, I bolted the door, which rarely happened. On the ranch, no one locked their doors. Today was an exception.

The French toast went into the oven, and I had an hour to think. That wasn't a good thing.

My thoughts swung from where we'd live if we did get married to strategies for avoiding a crying episode. I wasn't typically an emotionally demonstrative person. A father who yelled a lot taught me to shove my emotions deep inside and keep a straight face. When he ran out on our family, my coping strategies stayed in place. I was even keeled, and I ate food. Eating was my coping strategy.

Food was also how I showed love.

Fifteen minutes before Mad Dog was supposed to arrive, I pulled the French toast out of the oven and slid the pan of bacon onto the rack. Normally I started the bacon in a cold oven. Hopefully, it would turn out crispy.

When Mad Dog knocked, I focused on my breathing as I walked to the door. "Hi. Com—" I'd meant to tell him to come in, but the sight of the flowers in his hand rendered me speechless. I stared at them for a full second before glancing up to meet his gaze.

"Good morning." His smile was warm and bright.

I motioned him inside.

"These are for you." He held out the colorful bouquet. "And I brought a fruit tray. Didn't cut it myself. It's store bought."

"That's fine. Come in. The bacon will be ready in about

five minutes." I cradled the flowers, inhaling the floral scents of the assorted blooms.

No one had ever brought me flowers. I didn't even own a vase. I scanned the kitchen for something to put them in. A pitcher would work.

Mad Dog set the fruit on the counter, and as I added water to the pitcher, I was conscious of the fact that he was watching me.

"Thank you for the flowers. They're beautiful." I removed the paper from around the bouquet and arranged them, hoping he wouldn't notice the slight shake of my hands.

After setting the pitcher on the table, I pinched the skin between my thumb and forefinger. Who knew that I'd be using one of the techniques to avoid tears before we even talked about my offer? When the pinching didn't work, I blinked repeatedly.

"Ava." Mad Dog rested a hand on my shoulder.

The feel of his hand on me sent my thoughts right back to yesterday. Could he feel the shiver racing down my spine?

"Have a seat. What can I get you to drink? Coffee?" Forgetting that I wasn't wearing an apron, I wiped my hands on my shirt.

"Coffee, please." He remained standing.

I poured a cup, then set the sugar bowl and creamer on the counter. "Here you go."

He didn't touch the cream and sugar. "Ava, as I started to say yesterday, I don't want—"

I waved away what I knew was coming. "Don't worry about it. Let's just enjoy breakfast." I opened the oven and slid out the bacon.

"I don't want you to feel forced into something." He moved and stood beside me. "If there was no issue with my job, if lemon bars didn't exist . . . would you *want* to marry me?"

With an oven mitt still on my hand, I pressed it to my chest. I hadn't prepared for that question. Lying to a pastor seemed worse than a regular lie, but being honest risked embarrassing myself.

His soft brown eyes exuded kindness.

I could be honest with him. As self-conscious as I felt around Mad Dog, I trusted him. I worried more about hiding my own flaws. But honesty wasn't a flaw, right?

"I would." Feeling exposed, I turned away and shifted the bacon to a platter, waiting for him to respond.

One second of silence stretched into two.

After a deep breath, I turned back around.

He held out an open ring box. "Will you marry me?"

I had to replay the words in my head. "Did you . . .?"

He nodded.

I knew it was only to save his job, but my heart thudded as if he really wanted to spend forever with me. "Yes."

After slipping the ring out of its cushion, he reached for my hand. "Choices are limited when buying rings at eight in the morning, but I wanted to be able to give you something if you said yes. If you don't like it . . ."

Sparks danced where his fingers touched my skin. How was I going to keep my secret crush on my pastor a secret? That sounded nonsensical, but I knew this was for appearances. To make what I'd said true. To avoid scandal.

The blue topaz sparkled in the sunlight as he slid it onto my finger.

"I love it." My hand shook as I stared at it an extra second. Then I smoothed a stray hair back into my bun. "You're probably starving. Let me get breakfast on the table."

"That can wait a second." He opened his arms. "Come here."

This was going to be hard. It was easier to pretend he

didn't make my brain mush when he was across the room. When he touched me . . . I had no defenses against that.

I stepped into his arms. The tears that threatened when he'd shown up with flowers were nothing compared to what I was trying to hold back now.

What happened to my even keel and my ability to stuff my emotions?

His arms tightened around me. Tears slipped down my cheeks.

We were going to get married.

I was both overjoyed and terrified.

Wiping my eyes, I pulled away. "The French toast isn't as good cold."

"It smells delicious. What can I do to help?"

I handed him hot potholders. "Will you carry it to the table?"

"Of course."

We had a lot to talk about over breakfast. Then I had to figure out how to tell my friends and my brother that I was getting married . . . without sending anyone into shock.

CHAPTER 6

MAD DOG

*W*hile I devoured the French toast, Ava ate, playing with her ring between bites. I tried not to stare, but the gleam in her eye made me think she was happy. And every time she stopped eating to look at her ring, she followed the look with a glance at the flowers.

There was so much I hadn't said for fear of scaring her off. I could only hope my actions spoke loudly enough.

When she caught me watching her, her cheeks colored. And her smile set my heart racing.

I hadn't missed her tears when I'd handed her the flowers or when I'd hugged her after putting on the ring. I chose to believe they were happy tears, and by the end of breakfast, I was convinced.

"Ava, since our arrangement isn't typical, I think it's best that we are honest with each other."

"Of course." Her shoulders tensed.

I hadn't thought through how that would sound. "Not that I think you'd lie to me. But I want your opinion on all of this. Don't feel like you can't say something."

"All right." She shot me one of her intoxicating side glances without the slightest clue the effect it had on me.

Instead of sleeping, I'd spent half the night thinking about her and all that we'd need to discuss. "When would you like to get married?"

She pushed a piece of toast around her plate with her fork. "Whatever you think. I'm guessing the gossip will quiet down quickly if we do it soon."

"I agree. But I don't want you to feel rushed. Do you have any family far away that will need time to make arrangements to attend?"

She shook her head. "What about you?"

"My daughter will come. I'll call her as soon as we choose a date." I sipped my coffee. "I was thinking that I should talk to your brother . . . if that's okay with you."

Her eyes widened, but her head bobbed up and down. "What will you say?"

"That I want to marry you."

Ava sprang up out of her chair and walked into the kitchen. "I completely forgot about the fruit. It's just sitting here on the counter." She carried the tray to the table. "In two weeks. We could get married in two weeks. Make sure that works for your daughter."

"I'll check with her." I was quiet for a few minutes, giving her a chance to eat. Breakfast was delicious, and I looked forward to eating the wonderful foods Ava prepared. While I could cook, I only did on rare occasion.

"Where will we live?" Her voice quivered, and she glanced out the window.

I clasped her hand. "Unless you feel differently, I'd like to move in here."

It wasn't hard to figure out that Ava was deeply attached to the ranch. And I loved the idea of living on a ranch again. It was a life I missed.

The discussion about the house had no mention of bedrooms. Broaching the topic of room arrangements could wait until another day.

She nodded. "That's fine. It will be easier for me to continue working on the ranch."

"I don't want to interfere with that. Besides, Mrs. Beecham is my neighbor, and . . ."

Ava laughed, and it was a beautiful sound. "Say no more."

I'd buy a new house before moving Ava next door to Mrs. Beecham.

While we finished breakfast, Ava's smile was wide and genuine. I'd work every day to put that smile on her face.

"Thank you for cooking. It was amazing." I carried my dishes to the sink.

"You're welcome."

Even though I wanted to linger, I'd already scheduled lunch. And before I ran off to meet Reverend Saunders, I wanted to talk to Clint. Having him learn about the engagement by seeing the ring didn't seem like a good idea. I didn't know the man well, but he was definitely the protective type . . . and built like a wall. Having him angry with me was near the top of my list of things to avoid.

He had to know that Ava and I hadn't been dating. The engagement would be a surprise, and I wanted to be the one to break the news.

I leaned against the counter as Ava rinsed the dishes. "I'd love to stay and talk longer, but I'm going to see if I can catch your brother."

"That's fine. I need to head over to the main house in a minute and start cooking lunch." She stepped around me and put the rest of the food away.

"I'll call you later if that's okay."

She smiled. "I'd like that."

I walked toward the door, and Ava followed.

"Thank you for breakfast. It was better than anything I've ever made myself for breakfast. And I dare say better than any restaurant."

She twirled her ring around her finger. "I was happy to do it. I'm glad we talked here." Inching backward, she put space between us.

"Me too." I ached to pull her into my arms again, but I could read signals, so I shoved my hands in my pockets. "Thank you."

"For helping you?"

"For everything." I waved as I walked to my truck.

Ava stayed in the doorway until I drove away.

I'd been out to the ranch a few times and knew my way around enough to find the main house and the barn . . and now Ava's. I started my hunt for Clint at the main house, hoping someone there would know where I could find him.

With my heart pounding in my chest, I knocked on the door. I hadn't been nervous about asking Ava to marry me, but I wasn't as sure how this conversation would go.

To him, the announcement would come out of the blue.

Footfalls sounded inside, and then the door opened. Clint smiled. "Pastor, hello. You looking for Beau?"

"Actually, I was hoping to talk to you." I glanced down the hall, wondering if that cat would make another appearance.

Questions etched in his brow. "Sure." He motioned me inside.

I followed him through the living room into a game room.

He leaned against the pool table. "What's up?"

Being chatty wouldn't make telling him any easier. Since Clint was a man of few words, I opted to take a more direct approach. "I proposed to your sister. And I . . . since you are her brother, I thought . . ."

He shoved his hands in his pockets. If that was his way of

avoiding the temptation to take a swing at me, I appreciated the effort.

Clint blinked, and his brow pinched. "What did you say?"

"I want to marry Ava."

He rubbed his jaw. "You asked her?"

"I did. This morning." With my arms folded, I waited for the barrage of questions. "She made breakfast."

His hands came out of his pockets, and I prepared to duck.

But after scrubbing his face, he walked to a door, not the one we entered through. "Follow me."

I wasn't going to argue. He'd asked far fewer questions than I'd expected, and that made me nervous.

We walked into a large rustic dining room. Ava stood at the counter, tying on an apron.

Her gaze cut from Clint to me. I smiled with a confidence I didn't quite feel. I wasn't sure if her brother was happy with the news. The man would probably be amazing at poker.

Leaning on the counter, he looked Ava in the eye. "Do you *want* to marry him?" He hooked his thumb over his shoulder.

She pinched her lips together, then nodded. "I do." Then she shot me one of those looks again.

"This is a bit of a surprise." Clint looked from her to me.

I walked around the counter and put my arm around Ava. "I'm sure it comes as a bit of a shock. But you know what people say. Sometimes you just know."

His brow relaxed, and he smiled. "I expect you'll treat her well."

"Like the treasure she is." I didn't have to lie about that.

His gaze dropped to the ring on her finger. "I'll invite Joji over for lunch. She'll want to hear all about it. Are you staying, pastor?"

"Not today, but you'll be seeing me around a lot more." I

rubbed Ava's back before letting my hand fall. "I'll call you after my lunch meeting."

"Okay." She caught my hand, then inched up and kissed me.

I loved the kiss, but I didn't like the apology that flickered in her eyes. With her brother in the room, she was selling the story. I wanted her to kiss me for the sheer pleasure of it.

It would take time to win Ava's heart. Marrying her would be a good start.

CHAPTER 7

AVA

Clint would've noticed if I hadn't kissed Mad Dog goodbye. But I felt bad because displays of affection hadn't been discussed over breakfast. What if Mad Dog didn't want to be kissed? Later, when he called, I would apologize.

Before meeting Joji, Clint probably wouldn't have noticed whether I looked twice at Mad Dog, but she'd given him a new perspective. And that was great and all . . . until now.

My thoughts were not focused on cooking, and I grabbed the handle of a hot pan with my bare hand. "Dang it."

I ran my hand under cool water, then wrapped a clean towel around it. This would make cooking even more difficult.

"Ava Jackson!" Joji waved her arms as she ran across the room. "You haven't said a word, but I just knew he was sweet on you."

"What? Who?" The questions slipped out before my brain caught up.

She shook her head. "Very funny. What happened to your hand?"

"Grabbed a hot pan. I'm a bit distracted today."

"Of course you are. Tell me what to do." She lifted an apron off the hook and tied it on. "I'll finish lunch while you tell me all about it."

"You weren't going to wait for me?" Lilith grinned in the doorway. "Beau texted me, and I raced over. When is the wedding?"

News and wildfires both spread quickly in these parts.

"Two weeks, I think. He's going to check with his daughter to be sure she can make it."

I'd never met his daughter. He'd mentioned her before when we'd talked, but she lived in New York. She would probably be as shocked as Clint.

As thoughts connected in my brain, Lilith gave words to my realization.

"You're gaining a stepdaughter." She rubbed my shoulder. "You'll be great."

Lilith knew what it was like to be a stepmother. When she'd married Beau, she gained a stepson. And Garrett lived on the ranch, not in a different state. I had someone I could go to for advice.

Joji lifted my hand. "Let me see the ring. Why have you kept this a secret?"

"He only asked at breakfast." I tried to forget that getting married was all my idea.

"Not the wedding. She means Mad Dog." Lilith shook her head. "You hardly spoke to him at Joji's wedding. I'm amazed. That was only three months ago. I had no idea you were sneaking around with him."

"We—" I hated the idea that she thought I'd been sneaking around, but setting the record straight risked saying what I didn't want anyone to know.

He was only marrying me to keep his job. I was helping him.

I lifted the rag to see the damage to my hand. "Let me go put something on this. I'm hoping it doesn't blister."

"Go." Joji shooed me toward the door. "We'll feed the boys."

I slipped into the house and pulled out the first aid kit. I kept it fully stocked because I never knew when one of these guys would need something cleaned, wrapped, or bandaged. After spreading aloe vera on my hand, I covered it with gauze.

When the barstool in front of me scraped against the floor, I didn't look up, but I knew who it was. "I'm sorry if you were shocked by the news."

Clint chuckled. "I'll live. But I want to know one thing."

"What's that?" I stuffed supplies back into the kit.

"Two things, actually. Are you happy? And are you leaving the ranch?"

I pictured the flowers that were sitting on my table at home as I met his gaze. "I am happy." I felt almost guilty for feeling so happy. "As to the second one, that's quite a question from someone who moved off the ranch just a few months ago."

He rolled his eyes. "I'm not sure that moving to the goat farm qualifies as moving off the ranch. It's just on the other side of a fence."

"We decided that we'll be living here on the ranch."

Clint lifted an eyebrow. "Maybe we'll put him to work."

"Be nice." I waggled a finger in his face. "Please."

Beau walked up to the counter. "Clint is always nice." He dropped onto a barstool. "Do I need to start hunting for a cook and housekeeper?"

"I'm not leaving *or* quitting. I'm just getting married." I stuck the first aid kit back into the cabinet. "But if I need extra help, I'll let you know."

My phone buzzed as I walked back toward the dining room. I stopped and read the text from Mad Dog.

If you didn't have to cook for the guys at the ranch, I'd take you to dinner. Any chance you're free after?

When he sent texts like that, I entertained notions that he wanted to spend time with me just because. But he probably had more to discuss.

I hurried back to the dining hall. "Joji, I have casseroles in the freezer. If I move those into the fridge to thaw, will you serve them for dinner tonight? It should be easy."

"Sure thing. Have a big date?" She grinned. "I'm so happy for you, Ava. Really and truly happy."

"Thanks." I made room in the fridge for the casseroles, then scribbled out warming instructions. "If you really have this covered, I think I'm going to head home."

All the congratulations had guilt choking me. I'd trapped Mad Dog with my blunder, and now everyone was happy for me. Celebrating his entrapment seemed wrong especially when he was being so good-natured about it.

"Go ahead. We can cover lunch. I hope your hand feels better." Lilith studied me, and I could imagine the assumptions that were being made.

In the truck, I texted Mad Dog. *Joji and Lilith are covering dinner. I'm free.*

My phone rang before I pulled away from the main house, and I answered much too quickly. "Hello."

"Ava." The way Mad Dog said my name—with eagerness and excitement—made me feel like the first person chosen for a team. "Thank you for rearranging your schedule. I'll call again later to discuss a time."

"Sure. But I don't want to keep you. Reverend Saunders is probably waiting on you."

"He's running late. But I'll call you after and let you know what he said."

"I'm sorry for all the trouble." I put the phone on speaker and drove to my house.

"But with your help, the trouble is going to be resolved." Mad Dog said it so matter-of-factly.

"I hope so." I parked outside my house. "Want me to make dinner?"

"Not tonight. This time we'll go out to dinner. Oh, he's here. I'll call you." The call ended.

I went inside and crawled in bed. My lack of sleep had caught up with me, but when I tucked under the covers, my brain kicked into high gear. It took me more than an hour to fall asleep.

I couldn't have gotten more than a half-hour nap before a familiar soft knock sounded at the door.

Mason was about the only person who could interrupt my nap and not get a scowl. Maybe not the only person, but Mad Dog hadn't ever awoken me from a nap.

"Hey there! What can I do for you?" I waved at Kent who was standing near his truck.

"Daddy is going to go do some work in the pasture. He said I could go help Parker in the barn, but I wondered if you wanted to go swimming with me." He flashed a toothy smile.

"Sure thing, darlin'. Come on in. I'll run back and change." I stepped off the porch. "Kent, I'll keep him for a while."

"Thank you. You can leave him with Parker if something comes up. And the house is unlocked if he needs anything." Kent pointed at Mason. "Best behavior, buddy."

Mason nodded. "Yes, sir."

"Do you need to get your swimsuit?" I put a few cookies on a napkin.

He shook his head and grinned at the snack. "I put it on under my jeans just in case."

The little guy would live in the pool if we let him.

While he ate his snack, I changed into my swimsuit and

pulled on my coverup. I lifted the gauze on my hand. No blisters. The burn was still a bit sore, but not so painful that I couldn't enjoy a swim. The cool water would probably feel good.

After grabbing two pool towels, I walked out to the kitchen. "You ready?"

He nodded and wiped cookie crumbs off his mouth. Then he pointed at my phone which I'd mistakenly left on the table. "Mr. Dog called. I told him we were going swimming."

I quelled my panic. "His name is Mad Dog. Some people call him Pastor Miller."

Mason yanked off his shirt. "Mad Dog is a cool name."

"I suppose it is. You can undress at the pool. Go hop in the truck."

With his shirt half off, he ran out and climbed into my truck, telling me all about the new horse and his riding lessons. "And Miss Joji said that she'll teach me to feed her chickens and goats. I have to be careful of the llamas though. They spit."

"Yuck!" I stuck my tongue out and made a face, which sent Mason into giggles.

He chattered all the way to the main house.

As soon as the truck was in park, he was out the door.

"Don't get in the water until I'm over there." I slid out and grabbed the pool bag. It stayed fully stocked with sunscreen during the warmer months.

"Yes, ma'am." He ran around the house like someone was chasing him.

When I made it around to the patio, Mason was wrestling his jeans over his tennis shoes. I took the opportunity to return Mad Dog's call.

"Hi. Mason said you called." With my shoulder holding the phone to my ear, I dropped the pool bag into a chair.

"I did. I heard you were going swimming." Mad Dog sounded distant like he was in his truck.

"I'm keeping Mason busy. How was lunch?"

"Not bad. We can talk about it later. Enjoy your swim."

Not bad wasn't the same as good.

"All right. See you tonight." I tucked the phone in my pool bag.

Mason jumped into the water.

I picked up his clothing items, which were right next to the pool, then pulled off my coverup.

"Are you going to swim, Miss Ava?"

"I am."

"Will you do a cannonball? Please!"

Laughing, I kicked off my sandals. "Just one."

"Yay!" He clapped, flinging water all around him.

Standing at the edge of the deep end, I glanced toward the backdoor to make sure no one else was around. I never did the cannonball with an audience other than Mason.

He counted down. "Three . . . two . . . one . . . jump!"

As I launched myself in the air, Mad Dog walked onto the patio. If I could have backpedaled through the air, I would have. And in my panic, I completely forgot what to do, resulting in a spectacular and embarrassing belly flop.

Water slapped my face, stomach, and chest. I'd be one big bruise after this. Pool water sloshed from the impact. My not-so-skinny body could definitely make waves. Not in a good way.

If I had the ability to hold my breath for an hour, I wouldn't have risen above the surface. But since I required air to breathe, I had no choice. Every inch of the front of my torso stung.

And the impact had not only knocked the air out of me, but it also knocked the scrunchie out of my hair.

"Miss Ava, that was so cool!" The kid had no idea.

Mad Dog popped up out of the water beside me. "You okay?"

"I will be." After grabbing my scrunchie, I swam toward the edge of the pool, wishing I could vanish.

Getting out of the water meant he'd see me dripping wet in my suit. Not that he hadn't just seen me flopping onto the surface like a drunk walrus. I'd never actually heard of a walrus being drunk, but I imagined if it ever happened, it would look a lot like the display I'd just made.

I opted to stay in the water. "It just stings a bit. Mason likes it when I do cannonballs. But—"

"But I surprised you by showing up." Mad Dog rubbed my arm.

"A bit." I glanced at him, then looked away.

All my guesses about the muscles under his shirt were correct. And I knew that because his wet shirt was shrink-wrapped around every muscle.

Mason swam over to us. "I've never done a jump like that. Will you teach me?"

"I didn't mean to do that. It's called a belly flop because you land on your belly. And it doesn't feel all that great." Other parts of me ached more than my belly, but the five-year-old didn't need to know that.

He furrowed his brow. "Are you hurt?"

"I'm okay, darlin'. Go swim and have fun." I flashed what I hoped was a reassuring smile.

Instead of swimming away, he moved closer. "Who is that?" His whisper could probably be heard in the next county.

"This is Pastor Miller."

Mason grinned. "Mad Dog! I talked to you on the phone."

"It's nice to meet you in person, Mason." Mad Dog stuck out his hand.

After shaking hands, Mason dove under the water and swam away.

"It's not too late to change your mind." After embarrassing myself, it seemed only polite to give Mad Dog the opportunity to back out of the agreement.

He moved in front of me and put a hand on the edge of the pool on each side of me. "Because of a belly flop?"

I watched the water ripple in the space between us.

He touched a finger to my chin and lifted it until I met his gaze. "I didn't lie to your brother. I want to marry you."

Feeling extremely underdressed, I crossed my arms. Mad Dog wanted to keep his job, and I needed to help him do that.

"Okay, but I'm sorry you had to see that."

Creases appeared near the corners of his eyes. "Mind if I stay and swim?"

"Mason would like that."

Mad Dog inched closer. "Would you prefer I leave?"

I shook my head. "Don't leave."

He peeled off his shirt and laid it out in the sun.

Seeing him in a swimsuit was almost worth the embarrassment. Almost.

CHAPTER 8

MAD DOG

*S*howing up to swim hadn't gone as well as I'd pictured in my head. I'd wanted to talk to her about what had happened at lunch, but that would have to wait. Not all of it was great news, but since I'd gone on about honesty, I didn't feel it was right not to tell her.

The other reason I hadn't said anything was Mason. It was hard to have a discussion while chasing him in the pool.

He laughed and dove toward the bottom, swimming away from me.

Ava inched her way around the edge, and when she reached the stairs, I dove under the water, playing shark with Mason. If I'd known that having me see her in a swimsuit would make her so uncomfortable, I might not have come. But I wasn't sorry I did.

Mason giggled when I caught him.

"You've worn me out, kiddo. I'm going to go sit and talk with Ava."

His eyes narrowed and he moved closer. "Do you kiss her on the head or on the lips?"

What kind of question was that?

I bit back a laugh. "I'm not sure yet, why?"

He shrugged. "I think Mr. Clint liked kissing Miss Joji on the lips. That's why he married her."

It was easy to see how Mason would think that. Clint did kiss Joji almost every time she walked up to him. He wasn't shy about showing her affection.

"Well, I'm going to marry Miss Ava."

Telling Mason would make sure everyone knew.

He grinned and tapped his mouth. "Then you have to kiss her on the lips."

I'd definitely give Clint a hard time about this conversation later. Sometime after the wedding.

"Thanks for the tip." I stepped out of the pool.

Wearing her coverup, Ava held out a towel. "He has more energy than I ever dreamed of having." She laughed. "I'm guessing the cookies I feed him only fuel that."

"He's a fun kid."

"His dad is one of the ranch hands. We all pitch in to keep Mason busy while Kent is doing jobs that are best done without kids around." She sat down in a lounge chair and pulled her hair back into a bun. "How was lunch?"

I pulled a chair closer to her and stretched out, enjoying the sun. "Pretty good. Reverend Saunders is happy to marry us, but he asked that I not preach until after the wedding. He thought that would be best to let things calm down."

Ava grabbed my arm. "Then we shouldn't wait. What's the soonest your daughter can come?"

"We don't need to rush. It's okay."

Indignation burned in her gaze. "It's not okay. You didn't do anything wrong, and if it weren't for Mrs. Beecham, you wouldn't be trapping yourself to keep your job. I can only imagine what people will say when you don't preach on Sunday. It's just not right."

"Ava, I'm not going to rush *our* wedding for *those* people.

Reverend Saunders can preach. It's not a big deal." If there was one thing I'd learned as a pastor, it was that weddings took time to plan.

She chewed her lip a moment. "All right. If you're sure."

"Quite sure."

"Is a simple cake and punch reception okay with you?"

"Whatever you want is fine with me."

"I can bake the cake. Waiting will give me more time to find a dress. I'm sure Joji and Lilith will help me." She picked up her phone.

I clasped her hand. "You need to let someone else make the cake."

"But—"

"Ava, you make the best pastries in the entire world, but you cannot bake your own wedding cake. Please."

"I can see if Cami's friend has time to make one." She looked at my hand on hers.

"Cami? That name sounds familiar."

"She lived at Joji's place for a bit. Met her through Haley and Nacha."

"How could I have forgotten the chatty young woman who sat next to me at Nacha's second wedding?" I brushed my thumb on Ava's hand.

She laughed, but her gaze stayed glued to our hands. "She is chatty. Sweet girl."

"Let me call Poppy and see if she can be here the weekend after next." I stood and let Ava's fingers slip out of my hand.

She handed me my phone. "I picked up your stuff. Thankfully, your phone didn't break. You tossed it, didn't you?"

"When you hit the water, I shed almost everything but my swim trunks in a hurry."

She glanced at Mason, then back to me. "Thank you."

I nodded before walking to the edge of the patio and dialing.

The phone rang only twice. "Hi, Dad."

"Hey, sweetheart. She said yes."

"Wonderful! Have you set a date?" She sounded genuinely excited for me.

I wasn't sure how she'd react to the short timeframe. "Remember I said that we wouldn't wait very long?"

"Okay?"

"Could you be here the weekend after next?"

"In two weeks?"

I pulled the phone away from my ear, then rounded the corner, hoping Ava hadn't seen. I eased the phone back toward my ear.

"Are you there?"

"Yes, Poppy. I know it's soon, but if you can't make it, we'll wait until you can."

"Hang on."

I could hear tapping through the line. "Poppy?"

"Booked. I catch the redeye a week from Wednesday. And, Dad, I cannot wait to meet the woman who has you in such a hurry to get married."

"I think you'll love her."

"I'm sure I will. Clearly, you do." She laughed. "I need to go. I have to go tell my boss I need time off. I'll text you my flight info."

"Love you."

"You too, Dad."

Ava eyed me as I walked back toward her. "What did she say? Hopefully, she doesn't think . . ." She slapped a hand over her mouth.

"Poppy is excited. She booked her flight while we were on the phone. And what she thinks is true. I'm excited to marry you." I dropped into the chair beside her. "Do you need the evening to get a plan in motion? If you do, we can postpone dinner until Friday."

"If that's okay."

I nodded. "Do you need me to drag Mason out of the pool?"

Her gaze dropped from my face to my chest, and her cheeks changed to a soft pink. Then she shook her head. "Mason, sweetie, five more minutes. Miss Ava has some stuff she needs to do."

Mason climbed out of the pool. "Can I watch a movie?"

"You sure can. I'll even make you popcorn." She stood and handed him a towel. "Mad Dog, you are welcome to stay for dinner."

"I'll run home, then come back out. And I'll be ready for my honey-do list."

She smiled. "I'm glad you came to swim."

"Me too. I liked seeing you with your hair down." I decided that today was not the best time to take Mason's advice. Especially since he was standing right next to us.

She reached up and touched her wet bun.

"See you in a bit." I was really looking forward to being married to Ava.

CHAPTER 9

*B*ecause the casseroles for dinner were already prepped, I had extra time, so I made cupcakes in the main house. Keeping my hands busy didn't keep my mind from racing, but it kept me sane.

Not in a million years did I think I'd ever be planning a wedding . . . at least not my own. And now I had to plan one in two weeks. That wasn't a bad thing. The longer planning dragged out, the more to-dos were added to the list.

Joji laughed as she walked through the door. "You stood Mad Dog up just to spend time with stinky cowboys?" She pointed at the cupcakes. "And please tell me there is an extra one of those I can sample now."

"I was just about to frost them. They're finally cool enough. And Mad Dog is coming here for dinner. I have to start making a wedding plan." I'd been thinking about it a lot, but I needed to sit with pen and paper and write out an organized list.

"I'll take that as a yes, but I'll wait for frosting." She opened a drawer and pulled out a notepad and pen. "Number one. When and where. You're going to talk to Lilith about that, aren't you?"

"I planned to. Mad Dog likes the venue as much as I do, but he wants to pay."

Joji laughed. "That's not gonna happen. Number two. You need a dress. Something absolutely fabulous. And I think I have a lead on that. There is a lady that comes to yoga who is good friends with the woman who owns the bridal shop in that little town down the road. I'll see if I can snag you an appointment." She tapped away on her phone. "Is that okay with you?"

"Sure. I wasn't sure what I'd be able to get on such short notice."

"Y'all are planning the wedding without me?" Lilith dropped her large purse into a chair then bumped Joji's shoulder. "Did she say we could have one of those?"

Both ladies had radar for chocolate.

"As soon as I get two frosted." I gave the frosting a final mix before adding a dollop to the top of one cupcake. "Any chance there is availability at the venue? We wanted to get married in two weeks, but it doesn't have to be on the weekend. I know those book up."

Lilith pulled a planner out of her purse. "The weekend is full, but Thursday night is wide open. Would that work?"

"Yes. Just let me know how much it costs. Mad Dog said he'll write you a check." I handed over a cupcake.

"He will do no such thing. Consider it a wedding gift. What else am I going to get you? Pot and pans?" She motioned to the fully stocked kitchen. "You seem to have everything you need."

"Except lingerie. But we'll help you change that." Joji licked frosting off the top of her cupcake. "Number one is taken care of. I'm working on an appointment for the dress. What else?"

"Tons more to do. But we're here to help." Lilith picked up the pen. "Why in such a hurry? Eager to get your hands on him?"

I stopped mid slather and looked up. My cheeks had to be as bright as Joji's red hen. Before I could form words, I caught motion in the doorway.

Mad Dog waved. "Is this a bad time?"

I dropped the cupcake onto the counter. "Hi."

Joji whipped around. "We were just talking about you!"

"So I heard." He sauntered toward the counter, eyeing me.

How long would it be before I could read his expressions? Was he embarrassed? Upset? Amused?

"Want a cupcake?" I finished slathering frosting onto the neglected one.

"Don't mind if I do." He made that baked good disappear in only a few bites. "I didn't mean to interrupt."

"We're working on wedding plans." Lilith scribbled a date next to Joji's first item. "The venue has an opening a week from Thursday."

"Perfect." Mad Dog smiled.

"And it's our treat. In case you haven't noticed, we all kind of love Ava around here." Lilith added a few more items to the list.

"It's easy to see why." Mad Dog eased up beside me. "What can I do to help?"

I finished frosting the last of the cupcakes. "In that cabinet is a little metal tree that should hold all of these. You can put them in it."

He opened the cabinet and pulled out the cupcake tree. "Consider it done."

When the guys started arriving minutes later, everything was ready.

It wasn't unusual for me to be the last one seated. What was unusual was having everyone watch me until I sat down.

I took a seat next to Mad Dog. "Have all of you met Mad Dog?"

Grayson leaned forward. "We've all met him. And it's nice to have him here. But what I'm curious about is that ring on your finger."

Mason patted Mad Dog's arm. "Mr. Mad Dog is going to marry Miss Ava, but she isn't leaving. Are you?" His eyes widened as if the thought hadn't occurred to him before.

Mad Dog tousled the kid's brown hair. "I don't think I could talk Ava into leaving this ranch and all her cowboys. Not that I'd want to. So no, she's not leaving."

Multiple sighs of relief sounded around the table, and Grayson chuckled. "We all love you, Ava. And we'd miss your cooking."

"No need to worry. Mad Dog is moving into my place, so we'll be here on the ranch. Nothing will change." I motioned to the casseroles. "Let's eat before everything gets cold."

Only Mad Dog's address was changing. If I could nail that truth to the inside of my skull, maybe my emotions would play nice and not reveal my true feelings.

Beau held up his hand. "Before we eat . . . Mad Dog, would you like to say grace?"

Praying over the meal wasn't a regular thing here. Beau usually said a prayer at Thanksgiving and maybe at Christmas. That was it.

I hadn't intended to change life at the ranch by marrying Mad Dog. And I wasn't sure how comfortable Mad Dog was with being put on the spot.

"Sure thing. And I'll keep it short." If he was bothered, he didn't let it show.

Grayson chuckled. "I knew I liked you."

Mad Dog bowed his head and grabbed my hand under the table.

While he prayed over the food, I prayed that I'd made the right decision.

~

AFTER THE GUYS had cleared out of the mess hall, Mad Dog picked up a rag. "I'll get the table and the counters."

"You don't have to clean." I reached for the rag.

He grinned as I clasped his hand. "Would you rather I sit here and watch you clean?"

I shivered just thinking about him watching me. "Well, no." I let my fingers slip off his hand. "Clean away."

With his help, the dining hall was spotless in a short time. He leaned against the table with his arms crossed as I picked up my purse. He showed no signs of leaving.

"Do you . . . want to come over?"

He nodded. "I'd like that."

"I'll meet you there." I turned off the lights. How long would it take me to get used to having him next to me? Usually when I talked to Mad Dog, he was on the opposite side of the counter. And there were pies between us.

Once I arrived home, I waited on my porch as he climbed out of his truck. Kent and Mason waved, which sent me into a tizzy. Because of the audience, should I kiss Mad Dog? Or maybe some other indication of affection? I was giving way too much thought to how I should or shouldn't act.

Mad Dog waved at the guys before stepping onto the porch.

I shot another glance at Kent and Mason, trying to decide what to do. Mad Dog leaned closer. "Dinner was great tonight."

My gaze snapped back to him. "It was just a casserole." Much too flustered to land a kiss anywhere near his mouth, I shoved open the door.

Inside, he stood next to the couch until I sat down. "I'm glad they had an opening at the venue. It's a beautiful place."

"You are out there a lot."

"I am." Biting his lip, he rested his elbows on his knees. "This wedding . . ." He scrubbed his face. "It's not typical. And I—"

"Oh yeah." Even though I had no idea how he was going to finish that sentence, I agreed, ever eager to please.

He clasped my hand. "The way you looked at me this morning when your brother was there . . . when you kissed me . . ." He shook his head and inhaled. "I guess what I'm trying to say is that I don't want you to feel like you have to pretend. Not for me or for anyone. Obviously, when the minister says to kiss the bride, I think I should, but . . ."

"I understand." I'd pushed too far. But at least now I knew the boundaries.

He didn't want me to kiss him. That would be easier . . . as long as Lilith and Joji didn't ask questions.

The clock on the wall ticked away the echoes of silence.

"The prayer before dinner, is that just because I was there?" Mad Dog cocked his head, and crinkles formed near his eyes.

"I think so." I stared at a loose thread on the sofa. If I snipped it, I could probably keep it from getting worse.

The quiet between our one-line exchanges weighed heavily. It wasn't like this when we'd talked over pie.

Mad Dog spoke, breaking the uneasy silence. "You'll send me my honey-do list?"

How many conversations would it take before the awkward pauses disappeared?

"I will. It was nice having you at dinner."

"It wasn't as stressful as I imagined."

"Stressful?"

He chuckled. "I was in a room full of guys who would

take on anyone they thought was treating you badly. Being on the wrong side of that sounds painful."

"You don't treat me badly."

"Be sure to let them know that if it ever comes up." He winked. "Do you have any questions for me? We should get the deal-breakers out of the way first. Before we walk down the aisle."

I'd spent half the night thinking about how little I knew about the man. "I'm not sure what to ask. I know you have a daughter and that you're a pastor." And I knew he always scraped the apple filling out of his pie and never ate the crust, and I knew his arms were even better than I'd imagined. And if he had a tattoo, it wasn't visible when he was only in a swimsuit.

My gaze slipped downward.

I blinked, trying to get my thoughts back on safer subjects. Looking at his face would help.

"Here's the short version. I was widowed ten years ago. My only child is twenty-five and lives in New York. Five years ago, I decided to move back to Texas. My grandparents had a ranch not far from here, and growing up, I used to spend summers helping them. Of all the places I've lived, this part of Texas feels like home."

"I had no idea you spent time on a ranch."

"I miss it." He glanced out the window. "I made lots of happy memories working cattle with my granddad."

"Where did you live when you weren't on the ranch?"

"I lived up near Austin. After I married, I moved around a little, but mostly we were in Georgia. After Poppy moved to New York, there was no reason for me to stay in Georgia."

"What's your real name?" From there, I'd work my way to how he got his nickname. And if I felt really brave, I might even ask about tattoos.

Laughter echoed in the house. "You might not like my answer."

"How bad can it be? Mad Dog is a curious nickname for a pastor. For anyone really."

He nodded. "I'm named after my great grandfather. My given name is Madog. Pronounced a little differently than my nickname. It's Welsh. But the first time one of my elementary school friends heard my mother call me by my full name, I earned a new nickname, and it stuck."

"I'm almost afraid to ask about your middle name."

"My mother was fond of using family names. My middle name is Wolfe."

Putting the names together in my head, I bit back a laugh. "It must have been awful."

He shrugged. "I'd just growl when people teased me. It wasn't so bad."

"Do you prefer being called by your real name?"

"Haven't really thought about it. Only my parents and grandparents—the ones here in Texas—ever pronounced it correctly. And they've been gone a long time. To everyone else, I was Mad Dog. It's easier to just start with that rather than give a lesson on how to pronounce my name every time I meet someone new."

"I want to learn."

"Thank you."

I crossed my arms so he wouldn't see my hands shaking. "Do you have any questions for me?"

Smiling, he gave me a look that set my heart pattering. When he looked at me that way, I wished more than ever that I could read his thoughts.

"Not right now."

Not knowing what to talk about, I sprang up. "Can I get you coffee or pie or something? I can run to the main house and get you a slice."

"No thanks. You probably have a million things to do." He stood. "I'll be watching for my list, and I'll text you about plans for Friday."

Instead of a coherent answer, I nodded. I needed to stop doing that. No one wanted to marry a bobble head.

As he walked to the door, I kept my distance. My thoughts were tangled. One minute he was talking about not pretending, making it clear he didn't want affection to be part of the relationship. Then he'd look at me in a way that . . . that almost made me feel beautiful.

I really was sleep deprived.

"I'll call you tomorrow." He patted my shoulder before walking to his truck.

Standing in the doorway, I tried not to feel guilty about getting the better end of the marriage deal.

When his taillights disappeared from view, I closed the door. My pillow was calling my name.

The phone dinged as I climbed into bed. The text from Joji made sleep impossible.

My friend who has a friend who owns the bridal shop snagged you an appointment for the day after tomorrow. Isn't that exciting? Joji was just as excited as when she was choosing her own dress.

I don't even know what to say. That was the truth. Shopping for a dress made it feel real . . . and a wee bit terrifying.

Research was required. The woman at the dress shop would ask about what I wanted in a dress and what the ceremony would be like. Was 'two weeks' notice' an accepted wedding theme?

I think in this case the word was simple. As for the dress, I wanted something that would cover my less-than-skinny body but didn't look like a potato sack made of satin.

After two hours of watching clips from Say Yes to the Dress, I shut off my computer. Only months ago I'd gone with Joji to help her choose her dress. Based on my real-life experience and all the videos I'd just watched, I'd come to one major conclusion. I needed new undergarments.

Instead of me locking myself into a small room and wrestling with fabric until it slid over my lumps, there would be someone in there helping me get dressed. No wonder they often served alcohol at these appointments.

AFTER POW-WOWING with Joji and Lilith about tomorrow's shopping adventure, I drove into town. Alone. I didn't want help shopping for bras and panties. That was why I avoided all the stores where the sales staff hovered close and continually asked if I needed help.

Shopping for underwear in a discount store hopefully wasn't a bad omen for the wedding. It wasn't like Mad Dog would ever see what I purchased. It wasn't that kind of a marriage.

But it didn't seem fair that the cutest stuff was in the tiny sizes. I probably wouldn't have bought the little skimpy things anyway, but still. I settled on pieces that were practical —like panties with a hide-the-tummy panel—but pretty. Lacy but not see through, the underwear would be perfect for trying on dresses.

As I headed out of the lingerie section, a bodysuit that was extremely impractical caught my eye. One-piece lingerie would make a trip to the ladies' room much more complicated. I didn't need a black, sheer bodysuit. Those were meant to be seen. And the idea of being seen in it horrified me.

A woman bumped me with her cart, and I probably blushed because I'd been caught looking at lingerie.

"I'm so sorry for bumping you." She smiled and pointed at the racks. "I get so distracted by all the pretty lacy things."

She was more than a decade older than me.

Leaning in close, she smiled. "I don't model it for anyone anymore, but I still love how it makes me feel. Beautiful underneath. Don't you agree?"

I reverted to my bobble head move as I pulled the body-suit off the rack.

After glancing at the piece in my hand, she winked. "Live dangerously."

To me, living dangerously was trying a new pie filling.

"Thank you. I think I'll get this after all. It was nice meeting you."

"Verbena." She stuck out her hand. "And whoever he is, he's a lucky man." Off she went as if she hadn't just made my jaw drop to the floor.

I made my way to the register, feeling better about my purchases. If I could convince even a small part of my brain that Mad Dog was a lucky man for marrying me, then I wouldn't slink down the aisle, wishing to be invisible the whole time.

When I walked out of the store, Verbena was waiting on the sidewalk. "Would you like to go to lunch?"

Agreeing to lunch with a stranger probably qualified as living dangerously.

"Yes. Where would you like to meet?" Riding with a stranger was more dangerous than I was willing to chance.

She pulled out her phone and tapped on the screen. Showing me a map, she pointed at the name of a restaurant. "How about that place?"

"Perfect."

As I climbed into my truck, I glanced into my rearview mirror and saw her getting into the back of a limo. What had I gotten myself into?

CHAPTER 10

I glanced up when my office door opened. Reverend Saunders grinned. His habit of not knocking was an unwelcome change in my routine.

"I was hoping you were free for lunch." He scanned the room before letting his gaze rest on the spot where the rug once was. "Still smells like dessert in here."

"It does. And I already have plans for lunch today. Perhaps another time." I'd had lunch with him yesterday.

He didn't tire of my company easily. Or he was lonely.

"Sure. I'll stop in tomorrow." He waved as he walked out.

I was beginning to think I was his retirement plan. But I understood the loneliness. I'd been there. Moving back to Texas had helped. A little.

Being out at the ranch helped a lot. That wasn't the reason I'd proposed. I had genuine affection, respect, and love for Ava. I was eager to marry her. But living on the ranch felt like a bonus.

Running out to my truck, I checked the time. So far, I was on schedule.

My to-do list had arrived and asking my groomsman was

at the top of the list. Thankfully, Ava didn't care that I only wanted a best man and no other groomsmen. I also volunteered to handle the catering. The idea of only cake and punch had been nixed somewhere along the way. At lunch, I'd kill two birds with one stone.

When I stepped into the restaurant, Jeffrey waved from the far corner. I slid into the opposite side of the booth.

He pointed as the waitress made her way toward our table. "I have lots of questions, but we'll order first. Choose fast."

While he ordered, I scanned the menu, then told the waitress what I wanted.

As soon as she stepped away, he tapped the table. "You call me about meeting for lunch, but you choose a restaurant twenty-miles from my house. What's with all the cloak and dagger?"

"I'm trying to avoid town gossip. The news will get out eventually, but I'd like to give it a few days."

"That was vague. Spill it." Jeffrey wasn't known for unending patience.

"I wanted to ask you to be my best man."

He blinked. "What?"

"I'm getting married a week from Thursday, and I'd like for you to be my best man." I dropped the napkin into my lap. "If you'd rather not . . ."

"Just hold on. I didn't say I didn't want to, but I need some info. Who is the bride?"

"Ava."

He scratched his chin. "When did you ask her out? Last I remember, the two of you were stuck talking about pie and the weather because *you're a chicken*."

"Well, this chicken *proposed* to her."

"Have you gone on a date?"

"Not yet." I knew I'd eventually have to tell Jeffrey the whole story.

He sipped his coffee. "I still need more info. There are gaps in this story. I'm not saying no because honestly, you and Ava are a good match—at least from what I've seen—but this came out of the blue."

"I'll tell you, but I don't want this getting out. Ever."

"You make it sound serious . . . like she's just marrying you to help you out of a jam or something." Jeffrey laughed but stopped when he noticed that I wasn't laughing along with him. "You're kidding me."

"I wouldn't have asked if I didn't mean it. But the way we got to this point is unconventional."

He leaned back as the waitress set food on the table. "Now I get why I had to drive twenty miles to meet you for lunch. If the wrong people found out, everyone would be talking about it."

I waited until the waitress was far away. "I'll give you the short version. There was an incident with lemon bars, and some people from church found it scandalous and others made the assumption that Ava and I were planning to be married."

"So you just went along with that plan."

"The last few months, every time I came close to asking her out, she nudged the conversation in a different direction, but yesterday when I asked her to marry me, she said yes. I'm thinking my chances of her going out with me are better now." I doused my fries with ketchup.

Jeffrey shook his head. "That must have been some *incident*. In answer to your original question, sure. I'll dig out my suit—or do I need to rent a tux—and be your best man."

"Thanks. Suit is fine." I pulled out my notes. "And the other thing I wanted to ask you is if the restaurant could cater the reception. She has someone making the cakes. And I'm intending to pay."

"It'll be my gift. Ava is always feeding everyone. If you don't find someone to cater, she'll probably spend the week of her wedding making food." He chuckled. "But you chose well. That woman can cook."

"Coming from you that's a high compliment."

"The cooking part? I know good food. The choosing well? I'm not sure I'm the best judge, but I'm happy for you."

During the rest of lunch, we hashed out the menu, and I only texted Ava three times with questions. She hadn't answered yet.

Jeffrey kicked me.

"What was that for?"

He nodded toward the door. "Do you know who that is with your wife-to-be?"

"Ava's here?" My head turned like it was a weathervane in a windstorm.

"You didn't plan to meet here?"

"No. This is a pleasant surprise." I scooted out of the booth but stopped when Jeffrey kicked me again. "What?"

"The woman she's with has come into the restaurant before. Several times. Her son owns a tech company. Nice family. Completely loaded. I wonder how Ava knows her."

"Not sure." I hesitated. "I don't want to intrude on their lunch."

"Do I need to kick you again? You're engaged. At least say hello." Jeffrey rolled his eyes.

I hurried toward the door. "Ava, hi! This is a surprise."

A smile spread across her face. "I didn't know you were here. This is my new friend Verbena."

Verbena stuck out her hand. "We met in the lingerie department."

Ava's cheeks turned a bright red, and I decided then and there that I liked Verbena. A lot.

"Would you like to join us? Jeffrey and I were talking about the menu. And he agreed to be my best man."

Ava blinked. "You know The Cowboy Chef?"

Verbena started toward the table. "That man is talented."

I slipped my hand around Ava's. "I hope this is okay."

"Of course." She glanced toward the table where Verbena and Jeffrey were already chatting. "I didn't know she was going to say that."

"Not a problem. I hope you found something nice."

Ava's cheeks colored again, and I decided to drop that subject. Hopefully, it would come up again later. The way Ava tensed when I stepped close to her, I guessed it would be much later before she wanted to discuss lingerie with me.

CHAPTER 11

AVA

*J*oji waited until Lilith and I were both buckled in before backing out of the parking space. "That was so fun!"

I didn't exactly agree about the fun part because trying on fancy dresses and modeling them in front of people didn't even come close to my definition of fun. But all the uncomfortable modeling had been worth it. I'd found the perfect dress. Something simple and elegant that made me feel pretty.

Lilith leaned forward from the back seat. "The dress is amazing. Now we have to go find something for you to wear under it."

"That little shop in Stadtburg?" Joji glanced into the rearview mirror.

Lilith nodded. "That's what I was thinking. But let's have lunch first. Beau said he'd feed the guys."

"If he buys them all doughnuts for lunch, they'll be sick by dinner." I probably worried too much over how the guys coped when I wasn't around.

She laughed. "He won't. He'll probably get them tacos *and* doughnuts."

While Lilith and Joji chatted, I tapped out a text to Mad Dog. *I found a dress.*

He had other things to worry about, but I wanted him to know. Each item checked off the wedding to-do list got us one step closer to the altar. Was he excited about it? Or resigned?

No matter how much I tried to rein in my excitement, all the wedding planning had me giddy. Pretending like it didn't exhausted me.

I glanced down when my phone buzzed.

I can't wait to see you in it. One more week. His reply had me grinning like a hormonal teen. Technically it was a week from tomorrow, but I wasn't going to split hairs. If he was resigned, he was doing a great job of pretending.

When Joji turned off the engine, I looked up. "Oh, we're here."

"Someone has you distracted." She winked. "Let's go eat."

We settled into a table in the corner. And after the waiter walked away, Lilith folded her arms. "I want to hear how you went from not wanting to talk about how good-looking Mad Dog was to marrying him. Have you been sneaking off at night after the cowboys go to bed?"

Joji closed her menu and laid it on the table. "Clint asked a similar question. But oddly, he seems okay with the sudden announcement." She shrugged. "What set off the spark?"

I hadn't anticipated talk of sparks, so I flashed my most mischievous smile. "He's pretty hot. It's a wonder he doesn't spontaneously combust. And things just happened." There was my completely vague and absolutely truthful statement.

"Oh. Listen to you." Lilith nudged my shoulder.

"What was the moment? With Clint, it was in the barn

during the storm when he kissed me for the first time. That's when I knew I was in love." Joji sighed.

Lilith furrowed her brow. "Storm? In the barn? He was *on* the barn and the day was clear."

Joji grinned. "That's when Clint knew. But we aren't here to talk about my love story. I want to hear Ava's."

The waiter set our drinks on the table. "Have you decided?"

We ordered, and as soon as he walked away, Joji and Lilith focused on me. I could tell the truth . . . parts of it anyway.

"We always talked at functions. He likes my pies, and we'd chat when he came to the dessert counter. But things really got set into motion when I was helping him at church."

"*Helping* him? Ava!" Lilith raised her eyebrows.

My cheeks burned. "Just stop. Not like that. Anyway, I tripped, and he caught me." I closed my eyes. What would've happened if Reverend Saunders hadn't opened that door? "He's so kind."

Joji patted my hand. "It was obvious he'd been working to get your attention. I'm so glad you finally gave him a chance." She bit her lip. "I was afraid you were letting fear keep you from a happily ever after."

I shook my head, but I couldn't get out any words of protest. This wasn't a happily ever after. Not really.

Lilith leaned back as the waiter brought out food. "Where are you planning to honeymoon?"

"We aren't . . . we haven't talked about it."

She pointed at me. "After lunch we are going to get you something to wear under the dress and a few things to wear on your honeymoon. Even if you never leave the ranch. I can guarantee the guys won't be walking in without knocking."

Forcing a laugh, I stared at my plate. "Right."

Joji said, "I booked us a spa day on Friday. You mentioned

that you have a date that night, and we'll have you home in plenty of time."

"Spa day?" I popped a bite of food into my mouth, relieved that we were finished with the how-I-fell-in-love conversation.

She smiled without looking at me. "Manicures. Pedicures. Massage. And if you want me to add it, a *full* wax. Might be fun."

Food lodged in my throat. I didn't want to draw attention to myself, but not breathing overrode my desire to blend in. I swatted Joji's arm.

"She's choking!" Joji announced it to the entire restaurant.

A second later, I was out of my chair, and Lilith had her arms around me, squeezing my ribcage. Just as the waiter ran up, the piece of chicken launched across the table and hit him square in the chest.

"I'm so sorry." Coughing, I wanted to hide under my chair.

He shrugged. "That's not the worst thing that's ever happened. Are you okay? Should I call someone?"

"I'm fine. Thank you." I dropped back into my chair.

Joji bit her lip like she was trying to hold back a laugh. "I guess that was a no to the Brazilian wax."

In spite of my embarrassment, I laughed. Lilith joined in, and we looked like we'd spent the morning drinking.

"Definitely a no. Capital N. Capital O."

After this, maybe shopping for lingerie wouldn't be so bad.

JOJI HELD up a white lacy piece. "This corset laces up the back. You'd definitely need help getting out of this one. If you know what I mean."

Lilith rubbed my shoulder. "Your cheeks are redder than the cherry filling in your pies."

"You two make me want to hide in these racks." I moved away from Joji who was still giggling.

I walked up to the lady managing the shop. "I know I said I didn't need any help, but I changed my mind." I showed her a picture of the dress. "I need something to wear under this. Something that will hold my curves in the right place for a few hours."

"Right this way." She led me past Joji, then picked up the perfect piece. "I think something like this might work."

"Thank you."

"I'm Delaney. Just holler if you need anything else." She strolled back through the racks, fixing hangers as she went.

Lilith held up two slinky nightgowns. One red. One white. "One of these for the wedding night would be good."

"I'll think about it." I wanted out of the store before these ladies gave me any more suggestions. "I think I found what I needed. I'm going to check out."

"We'll be out in a minute." Joji jingled her keys. "Want these?"

I plucked them out of her hand. "Have fun shopping."

After paying, I walked toward the door.

Lilith waved. "Are you sure you don't want to get something for after the wedding?"

Turning to face them, I shook my head. "I'm not shopping for that with y'all."

Joji held up a skimpy little thing that was almost completely see through. "What about this?"

"Bye!" I backed out the door and froze when I collided with someone. "I'm so sorr—" The word caught in my throat when I saw who it was.

Mad Dog grinned. "Well, hello." He glanced down at the bag. "Can I see what you bought?"

"Absolutely not." I tucked the bag behind my back.

He stepped closer. "I'll just have to be patient."

Like Job was patient. Because I had no plans to let him see what was under my dress for a very long time. Until the sun burned out and life ceased to exist. Yeah. Probably until then.

I braved a look at his face, knowing my cheeks were as red as cherry-pie filling. "We keep bumping into each other."

"You caught me on my afternoon doughnut run. I don't indulge every afternoon, but today I had a craving." He glanced up as the shop door opened. "Would you like to join me? I'll drive you home."

"I'd like that." After the words had spilled out, I thought about all that needed to be done on the ranch. "But I should probably . . ."

"You should absolutely not." Joji held out her hand. "I need my keys. The ranch will survive one day without you."

I handed over the keys. "All right. There are casseroles in the freezer."

"Thanks, Joji." Mad Dog slipped an arm around my waist. "This is an unexpected treat. I might ask you some questions."

"What do you want to know?"

"Patience. Let's get our doughnuts first."

With his arm around me, we walked into the little shop. His touch had every nerve in my body doing the Macarena. But if I shivered now, he'd know it. And how would I explain that?

Since falling into Mad Dog's arms, I'd seen him every single day. And my attraction had jumped from a manageable level to a craving. His soft brown eyes and those strong arms were going to be part of my life.

We stepped into the shop, and I stared at the glass case. Deep inside, I was a tiny bit jealous of Lilith and Joji and wished for a reason to buy pretty things.

Even if Mad Dog loved me and I loved him back, I wasn't sure I could ever voluntarily let him see me in something like what Joji pulled off the rack. Shoot. I couldn't imagine letting him see me in anything in Delaney's shop.

Breath tickled my ear. "What do you want?"

I had no idea how to answer that question.

CHAPTER 12

MAD DOG

I popped the top off two bottles of a local pale ale and handed one to Jeffrey. "How was the restaurant business tonight?"

"Busy. It's probably good y'all couldn't make it tonight." He rested his boots on my coffee table. "Why'd you cancel?"

"Ava seemed distracted by wedding plans, so I offered to move our reservation. She jumped at the idea. So . . . I spent the Friday night before my wedding alone."

"What am I? Chopped beef?"

"You know what I mean. And I appreciate you coming over." I jumped up when the oven beeped. "Food's ready."

"Smells good. You didn't make it, did you?"

"Ava sent me home with a casserole." I served up two plates of food.

Ava had become more and more distant as the week progressed. I worried that by Thursday she wouldn't even be talking to me anymore.

He picked up a plate. "What's eating at you?"

"You know how when we were younger and we'd flirt,

some girls would act like they didn't notice because they weren't interested. But there were other girls who really didn't seem to notice. It was as if they didn't expect anyone to be interested, so they were blind to the flirting. Anyway, Ava is the second kind." I sighed.

"There is a third option you might want to consider."

"What's that?"

He took a swig of his beer, timing his pause with intention. "Maybe you are just bad at flirting."

"You aren't helping."

Rolling his eyes, he shook his head. "She's marrying you. Whatever is going on, you'll have time to figure it out." He picked up his fork and then put it down again. "Besides, I'm good at flirting, but I can't get anyone to marry me, so maybe being bad at flirting isn't a bad thing."

"Maybe." I lifted my bottle. "To bad flirting."

"And to finding the right woman." He clinked his bottle against mine.

POPPY WALKED out of the airport, smiling from ear to ear. She'd gotten the morning person part of her personality from her mom. I was still wishing I'd gotten up early enough to have coffee before leaving the house.

I grabbed her bag. "Thanks for coming."

"Seriously, Dad? There is no way I'd miss your wedding. When do I get to meet her?"

"We're going out to the ranch to have breakfast. That's where she lives." I tossed her bag into the back seat.

"She has a ranch?"

"No, no. She works as a housekeeper and cook. You'll get to meet *everybody* at breakfast. Not just Ava."

"Ooh! Cowboys. If I'd known, I might've spent more time with my makeup . . . or actually put some on." She flipped the mirror down. "Yikes. I think it's useless. I didn't get enough beauty sleep."

As the dad, I said what was required, but that didn't make it any less true. "You are beautiful with or without makeup. And I'm not sure you need to worry about the cowboys. They live here. You live in New York."

"True, but what's the harm in making new friends?" Mischief oozed from her every word.

Having a single daughter wasn't for the faint of heart.

On the way to breakfast, she caught me up on her life in the big city. I called her often, but I loved hearing the stories in person. And I really loved seeing her happy.

When we parked outside the main house, she jumped out. "I'm going to need some boots. You're going to live here?"

"Ava lives down that road. Not too far from here. It's an easy walk."

"What are you going to do with your house?" She stuffed her hands into her back pockets, which she did when she was nervous.

"Probably rent it out."

As we walked toward the dining room, she watched the ranch hands file in.

What was I thinking bringing her to breakfast?

"Mr. Mad Dog!" Mason bolted away from his dad and headed toward me.

I scooped up Mason. "Hey there. This is my little girl. Poppy, meet Mason. Mason, this is Poppy."

He wriggled down and stuck out his hand. "Hi. You have a cool name too. Like your dad."

"Thanks." Poppy beamed. "Do you work here?"

Mason bobbed his head. "Sometimes I help my dad when

he's taking care of the cows. And Parker teaches me about the horses." He grinned as Kent walked over. "That's my dad."

"Hi." Kent tipped his cowboy hat. "Sorry about that. He's been talking about you since you played with him yesterday." He looked at me then shot a glance at Poppy. "I'm Kent, Mason's dad."

"Poppy Miller. His kid." She poked my arm. "This is a nice ranch. I'd love to see more of it. The cows. The horses. And whatever else is roaming around."

Mason pointed off into the distance. "After breakfast, my dad can take you out to the pasture. There are lots and lots of cows. Big ones."

"If I have time, I'd like that." Poppy shoved her hands back into her pockets again.

I rubbed her shoulder. "Come on. I want you to meet Ava."

Mason ran along beside us. "Miss Ava is the best cook in the *whole* world." He threw his arms wide open. "She makes pies and cookies. And she does the best cannonball. But she only does it when no one else is at the pool. Except me and Mad Dog." He whipped his head toward the entrance. "I smell bacon." Off he went.

"Excuse me. I'm going to make sure he leaves some for other people." Kent hurried away.

Poppy laughed. "Mason seems like a sweet kid."

"He is. And Kent is nice too." I watched for her reaction.

She shook her head. "Just stop. I'm going home after the wedding."

I laughed. "What happened to making new friends?"

"Introduce me to Ava. That's why I came." She walked into the dining room, and though it was a subtle move, she scanned the room.

Mason waved. "I'll save you a seat, Poppy."

Ava looked up from the counter. Pale, she'd probably slept less than I had.

"Ava, this is Poppy."

"Hi. Your dad and I are so glad you came." She stepped around the counter, then hesitated a moment before opening her arms. "It's wonderful to meet you."

Poppy hugged Ava. "Nice to meet you too. My dad has mentioned you often, so I can't say this is a total shock."

I'd mentioned Ava during our phone calls, but I'd never said anything that would make Poppy think Ava and I were dating.

The look of surprise on Ava's face was priceless. It probably matched mine.

"Well, good. Grab a plate. There's plenty. And if you need anything else, just let me know." Ava jumped back into serving mode and retreated to safety behind the counter.

Now that I knew Poppy and Ava got along—not that I had any doubt they would—I was even more excited about the wedding. Maybe then Ava wouldn't keep a counter between us whenever she could.

THAT EVENING while Ava looked out at the rolling hills bathed in moonlight, I studied her. She'd stayed an arm's length away from me all day, and I worried she was having second thoughts.

"I'm amazed at everything you've gotten done."

She tucked a stray hair back into her bun. "I had help. Poppy, Joji, Lilith . . . even the guys."

"It's like one big family here on the ranch." I was looking forward to moving here for that reason. "If I didn't like Mason so much, I might be jealous. Poppy has spent more time with him than she has with me." I laughed, then glanced at the other house. "He's currently showing her his rock collection."

Ava smiled. "I'm always emptying rocks from his pockets when I do the laundry."

"You do everyone's laundry?"

"Not all of them. But most." She crossed her arms, not at all acting like someone excited about getting married.

I stepped closer. "Ava, if you don't want to do this . . ."

She gave me another one of those side glances that set my heart pounding. "I want to."

The door opened at the other house. And I could hear Poppy talking, but she hadn't moved off that porch.

"Sounds like she's about to head this way. I guess I'll see you in the morning."

Ava shook her head. "It's bad luck." Her shoulders fell. "I guess that's silly. I'll be up by five. Y'all are welcome at breakfast."

"*I* won't be awake at five. I'm not sure how you are surviving without sleep."

"I just figure I'll sleep eventually. Last night, I used the time productively and readied the guest room for you. Cleaned out the closet and everything." She kept her gaze fixed on the landscape.

The guest room? That was news I hadn't expected. I was still excited about the wedding, but less so about the wedding night. While I didn't expect intimacy right away, I had assumed we'd be sharing a room.

"You didn't have to go to all that trouble. We'll figure it out." I clasped her hand when I heard Poppy coming. "I'll see you tomorrow . . . at the altar."

And if Ava hadn't inched backward, I would've done more than squeeze her hand.

"Night, Madog." She did her best to pronounce my name the way I'd shown her.

"Goodnight." I walked off the porch and waited by the truck as Poppy ran up to say goodbye to Ava.

While it was tempting to make declarations about how I felt, then kiss her until her toes curled, I knew that wasn't the best choice.

After the wedding, I'd woo my bride . . . slowly and intentionally. From the guest room.

CHAPTER 13

AVA

The day of my wedding, I was a bundle of nerves. I sat in front of the mirror as Lilith and Joji fussed over my hair and makeup. Being the center of attention made me uncomfortable. Especially given the circumstances. Sure that my eyes would give away the truth—that Mad Dog was marrying me to avoid being fired—I avoided eye contact with everyone.

One thing I couldn't take my eyes off of was the dress. I loved the simple, elegant gown I'd chosen, but I wouldn't be swallowing my bite of cake for fear that would cause the zipper on the back to burst open. Sacrifices had to be made.

It was a small price to pay for looking pretty on my wedding day.

Joji lifted my hair up, then let it hang down. "Your hair is gorgeous, Ava. I know you always wear it up, but today, I think it would look fabulous if you wore it down."

Lilith nodded. "I agree."

"I'm not sure." Biting my lip, I stared at my reflection and remembered how Mad Dog had said that he liked seeing it down. That swayed my decision. "Don't put it up."

"Yay!" Joji clapped. "Mad Dog is going to love it. Speaking of things Mad Dog is going to love, Lilith and I left a little something for you on your bed. We bought it at that little shop after you left with Mad Dog."

A surprise gift. How fabulous. That was what I got for not locking my door.

"Oh, thank you." Now I had one more thing I could shove in a drawer that would never be seen again.

As the minutes ticked by, they transformed me into a better-looking version of myself.

The hard part was sitting alone with my thoughts as Joji and Lilith dressed for the wedding. With so little time, they'd each chosen a dress suited to them. The colors weren't the same, but they didn't clash.

When the little motor cart arrived to drive us to the chapel, I started frantically pinching the skin between my thumb and forefinger. I needed the technique to work. Crying now would undo all their effort.

Clint drove us to the chapel, then climbed out. "You ready, Ava?"

I nodded, hoping that when it came time to speak during the ceremony, my voice would actually work.

Joji and Lilith fussed over my dress, then one by one they hugged me.

"You look beautiful." Joji squeezed my hand.

Lilith pointed at me, then at Clint. "Remember to walk slowly." Then she started down the aisle.

Joji flashed a thumbs up before taking her turn.

My brother held out his arm. "If his feelings weren't obvious, I'd have given you a hard time about how fast all of this has happened. I know you'll be happy. And I'm glad you aren't moving away."

Mad Dog had everyone convinced, but I knew the truth. However, I cared for him enough to promise to love him. It might never be the kind of love Clint and Joji had or the kind that Beau and Lilith shared, but Mad Dog and I shared a mutual affection. Hopefully, that was enough.

The doors opened, and Clint patted my hand before stepping into the chapel.

Reminding myself to breathe, I looked to the front . . . to Mad Dog. His smile drew me to him.

No matter what craziness had gotten us to this place, I trusted him.

Mostly.

And if I could make it through the kiss at the end of the ceremony without fainting, Mad Dog and I could go back to being friends. Married friends.

At the front, Clint shook Mad Dog's hand, then Mad Dog clasped my hands.

Although I just wanted to look into his eyes throughout the entire ceremony—because so far today, that was the only thing that calmed me—I felt obligated to give my attention to Reverend Saunders as he spoke.

I turned to face him but glanced over at Mad Dog. He winked and was probably thinking of lemon bars. And now I was thinking about lemon bars and being on top of him.

My cheeks burned.

Finally, the reverend stopped prattling on about love and whatnot, and Mad Dog and I faced each other, ready to say the iconic words that I never thought I'd say . . . to anyone.

He reached up and brushed my cheek. I couldn't pinch myself and hold his hands, and because of that, tears were breaking free.

When Reverend Saunders told Mad Dog he could kiss the bride, my heart stopped. This part I wasn't ready for.

His hands moved to my waist, and softly, he pressed his lips to mine. Instead of breaking away quickly, he pulled me closer.

I melted.

This was the moment I wanted to remember. Because I didn't expect it to happen again. Not after what he'd said about not pretending.

But I had my moment, and the memory of it would always be mine.

After breaking the kiss, he smiled, then kissed me again so quickly it caught me by surprise. "Ready?"

Nodding, I looped my arm around his.

Arm and arm, we strolled out of the chapel as Mr. and Mrs. Madog Miller.

BECAUSE THE WEDDING WAS SMALL, I enjoyed the reception. With only our friends and family there, it was easy to have fun.

After our celebratory dance, Mad Dog and I cut the cake Cami's friend had made. And as much as I hated to admit it, it was better than any cake I'd ever baked.

Following tradition, we fed each other a small piece. And despite the risk to my zipper, I swallowed the bite.

Chuckling, Mad Dog whispered in my ear. "Lemon filling was a nice choice."

I didn't want to think about how red my cheeks were. "I asked Cami to handle it. She chose the flavor. I wasn't trying to . . . you know."

He laughed. "It's delicious."

"Better than mine, but don't repeat that." I wiped a bit of frosting off the side of his mouth. "I think it's time to toss the bouquet."

"After we toss stuff, we'll get you home. You've got to be exhausted."

"A little."

The single ladies gathered together. With my back to them, I tossed the bouquet of gerbera daisies behind me.

When I saw Mad Dog's face, I knew who'd caught the bouquet. Seeing him as a dad was endearing.

He shook his head as he walked up to me. "I'm not even ready to think about that. I know she's an adult, but still."

"Sorry. I promise I didn't plan it." I sat down on the stool and held my breath.

Mad Dog knelt in front of me. "I didn't think you had."

The conversation wasn't enough to distract from the feel of his fingers grazing my thigh as he reached under my dress and slid the garter down my leg. The whole time his gaze held me captive.

If I kissed him right now, it wouldn't be pretending. Not for me at least.

He stood. "Everyone ready?"

The ranch hands who were gathered on the floor laughed. "Yep."

The garter flew into the air, but I didn't know who caught it until I saw Poppy's face.

Too bad New York was so far away.

EXHAUSTED and tired of being on display, I rubbed Mad Dog's arm. "It all turned out."

"Everything was perfect. You ready to head home?"

"I think so. This is fun, but I'm tired."

After saying our goodbyes, Mad Dog drove us back to the house in the little motor cart.

"What did Poppy say about catching the bouquet?" I was glad I'd already mentioned the guest room. Going to the house after the wedding would've been awkward otherwise.

"Nothing. She just grinned." He stopped the engine and

jumped out. "I think she was more interested in who caught the garter."

I gathered up my dress and walked onto the porch. "Did you bring a bag?"

"It's in my truck. I'll grab it."

In my bedroom, I closed the door before Mad Dog saw what my friends had left on the bed. Joji and Lilith must've had great fun shopping for that. I couldn't imagine wearing the small, lacy piece . . . especially in front of anyone else.

I shivered at the horror.

The entire little number was made of sheer fabric and lace. What was the point of wearing something sheer?

It didn't hold in any rolls, and it didn't hide them either.

Reaching behind me, I tried to get the zipper down on the back of my dress. It wouldn't budge. It didn't help that I could only reach it with the tips of two fingers.

After several tries, I swallowed my pride and opened the bedroom door. "Will you help me?"

"Of course." He stood in the hall, looking like every woman's dream come true. His tie hung loose, and his sleeves were rolled up.

I turned, giving him access to the zipper. "I can't unzip my dress."

"Let me help." He had no trouble getting the zipper to slide down, which made it seem like I'd been fibbing just to get him to undress me. "There."

"Thanks." I launched into the bedroom and closed the door.

I was self-conscious of the way I looked in my clothes. I hated the idea of him seeing me in less.

After changing into flannel pajamas—Lilith and Joji would've been horrified—I walked out to the living room.

Still in his suit pants and dress shirt, Mad Dog sat on the couch.

"I haven't even shown you the room. I'm sorry."

"I guessed it was the first room because the closet is empty. And there is a bed in there."

"Right." I sat at the opposite end of the sofa.

He scooted closer. "Are we still on for dinner tomorrow night?"

"Sure. Yes. Let me know what you like to eat. I can make something different for you than what I make for the guys. I don't mind."

"I want to take you to dinner. We'll go out and celebrate."

Why did I feel as nervous as if he were asking me out? "Okay. I'll have Beau order pizzas for the guys."

"Does it bother you to have me here?" He leaned forward and stared at the coffee table.

Since lying was bad, I had to choose my answer carefully. "I've been alone a long time, and I don't like how . . ." I quit talking before I was too honest.

"I think you're beautiful." He stood, then leaned down and kissed my cheek. "Goodnight, Ava."

That compliment would give me sweet dreams for a week. "Night."

CHAPTER 14

MAD DOG

There was a gleam in Ava's eye when I complimented her, but hesitation was mixed in. It was as if she could hear the words but couldn't believe them.

I left her sitting on the couch in her cute flannel pajamas, which were not typical wedding-night attire. If I had any hope of sleeping, I needed a cold shower.

After my shower, I tucked in bed, but I wasn't having any luck going to sleep. Based on the sounds in the kitchen, Ava was awake too.

I pulled on a shirt before walking out of my room. "Hey there."

"I'm so sorry. Did I wake you?" She closed the oven door. "I couldn't sleep, so I baked a cake. I would've made a pie, but making a pie crust is a lot of work."

"It wasn't you. I was just awake."

"Can I get you something? Coffee probably isn't a great idea right now. But I have tea, the ingredients for hot cocoa, and I have a bottle of wine."

"A glass of wine sounds good." I sat down at the table.

She poured two glasses. "The cake won't be ready for a bit. Let's sit in the living room."

I followed her to the living room and sat down on the couch, leaving a small gap between us. "How did you end up working at the ranch?"

"Beau's parents knew I needed a job, and they hired me to cook and help clean. It wasn't as if his mom didn't do anything. She cooked and cleaned, and I helped. After she died, I took over all the cooking and cleaning." Ava snuggled into the corner of the sofa, sipping her wine.

"It seems like a big job for just one person."

"It's become a bigger job lately. Beau keeps offering to hire someone to help, but I don't know."

"You should let him. You seem to like the cooking more than the cleaning."

"True. I love being in the kitchen." Swirling the wine around in her glass, she stared at the deep red liquid. "I bet it's hard with Poppy living so far away."

"In a way. We talk on the phone a lot. She indulges me and keeps me updated on her life."

"What's your favorite food?" Her eyes twinkled with excitement.

"Favorite is such a limiting word. I love food. All kinds."

"Surely there is something you miss having or used to have as a kid that you'd love to have again." She nudged me with her foot.

The gesture was playful and almost intimate. Other than our interactions at the wedding and reception, she rarely touched me. Touching was a good thing . . . even if it was only with her foot.

"Meatloaf. Meatloaf and fluffy mashed potatoes with brown gravy. I haven't had that in years." I patted her foot. "What about you? What's a favorite food? Something you don't make for yourself or get very often."

"Don't laugh."

I crossed my heart.

"Peeps. I love anything marshmallow, but when they are covered in sugar, I'm in love. Once we roasted them. It's my favorite way to have them." She finished the last of her wine.

"I bet those are good."

"So good. The sugar gets like glass on the outside, like the topping on crème brûlée."

I went into the kitchen and picked up the wine. "Refill?"

"One more glass."

After refilling both glasses, I settled back on the couch. "Any place you've always wanted to visit?"

She smiled at me over the rim of her glass. "Anywhere. I've never been out of Texas."

"Really? Maybe we'll have to change that." I drank a few sips of wine. "Did you grow up near here?"

The twinkle in her eye went out, and she chewed her lip. "Yes."

I rubbed her foot. "You can tell me to be quiet if you don't like my questions."

"It's okay. I just don't talk about it much. Growing up, I mean." She tilted her glass up and let the last drop slide into her mouth. "My father wasn't a nice person. And after he left us, things were really tight." She trailed a finger along the rim of her empty glass. "And high school is a hard time to not have any money. Especially when everyone knows you live on a goat farm."

"That must've been difficult."

She nodded. "After high school, Clint got married, but he helped us as much as he could . . . even though his wife gave him fits for it. Then our mother died a few months after that. When Beau's parents offered me a job, it was a lifesaver. This was the first place I'd ever felt completely safe. You were right when you said that people here on the ranch are like family. It's true. Beau is like a brother, and the ranch hands don't care about my extra pounds. They love me because I feed them." She wiped her eyes. "And then Mason showed up. He's probably the closest I'll come to having grandkids. Those are all the reasons I stay."

"Thank you for letting me join the family." I picked up the wine bottle, and she held out her glass.

"You're kind in the same way Beau's parents were. I notice things like that."

After filling up her glass halfway, I topped off my glass. "I try. I'm not always good at it. But I try."

"You are better than I am. I would've told Mrs. Beecham where she could go multiple times over. I don't like that woman."

"Because she isn't kind."

"I've known too many people like her. Mean people who use words as weapons and who find joy in making others feel worthless." She patted her hip. "But I've insulated myself."

I'd found the way to get Ava to talk about something other than pies and the weather, but downing an entire bottle of wine every night didn't seem wise.

The oven timer went off, and she jumped up. I didn't get my feet out of the way fast enough, and she tripped and landed in my lap.

Instead of the horrified reaction I expected, she giggled. Then she stopped and looked at me before exploding into another fit of giggles. "I haven't had this much to drink since I don't know when."

I helped her to her feet, then walked with her to the kitchen. "Let me get the cake out of the oven for you."

"Put this toothpick in the top."

I stuck the toothpick into the top of the cake as instructed.

She burst out laughing. "Pull it out. You don't leave it in."

I made sure she had a firm grip on the counter before yanking the toothpick out of the top.

After snatching it out of my hand, she grinned. "It's clean. The cake is ready. I'll get us plates."

We sat down, and she touched my hand. "Do you like it?"

I popped a bite of cake into my mouth. "Wow, Ava. This is the best chocolate cake I've ever tasted."

Her smile widened. "Good."

We ate in silence for the first few bites.

"This house was where Beau and his family lived when I first came. They let me live in that bedroom where you're staying. They didn't have extra cabins back then." She filled two glasses with water, then returned to the table. "But it was hard having no place to myself. On Sunday afternoons, I used to cross the river and go read in the old cabin. It was a complete mess the first time I went over there. And I spent hours cleaning it."

"It was your getaway."

"After Beau's parents died, I didn't have time to go out there often. And since the bridge washed out in a storm, I haven't even tried to get over there."

"I hope my being here isn't ruining your quiet space."

"No." She shook her head. "I feel better now that we've talked. It seems less awkward."

"I'm glad."

She picked up our empty plates. "I need to sleep. I have to be up in three hours."

When she stepped away from the sink, I pulled her close and hugged her. "Thank you for the cake."

She giggled again. "Now you can tell people we were up really late on our wedding night." After rubbing her face, she shook her head. "I need to stop talking now."

"Goodnight." After making sure she made it safely to her room, I crawled in bed.

Now I knew the truth. She'd insulated herself. I was on a quest to break through her insulation. And to do that, I needed to earn her trust.

CHAPTER 15

AVA

I rolled out of bed at five, threw on jeans and a t-shirt, and tiptoed out of the house. After we'd stayed up so late, I wanted to let Mad Dog sleep.

In the mess hall kitchen, I pulled casseroles out of the fridge. I'd have to replenish my stash soon.

Before Beau married, I made breakfast in his kitchen. He'd already built this second kitchen and dining room, but he'd wander into the kitchen in the mornings. The company was nice. But now I cooked all the meals in this dining hall kitchen. Married couples needed privacy, and I didn't need any surprises.

While the ovens preheated, I made coffee. I'd need lots of that today.

The door to the game room creaked, and in walked Lilith.

She shook her head. "Why are you here?"

"I'm making breakfast."

She leaned over the counter. "Ava, you got married last night. No one expects you to make breakfast."

I hadn't thought about how it would look for me to go on as if life hadn't changed. "I . . ." I shrugged. There was nothing

I could say that wouldn't give away more than I wanted Lilith to know.

She watched as the coffee filled the carafe. "When I was in the doughnut shop picking up the cake, I overheard a woman telling a story. It seems the pastor was caught rolling around in a batch of lemon bars with a woman. And there was talk that he was going to be dismissed. I ignored it as small-town gossip, but now I'm curious."

I pulled creamer out of the fridge, then filled a mug with coffee. "It was an accident. I tripped."

"You weren't intentionally rolling in dessert with the pastor?"

"How can anyone who knows me think I would ever do something so outrageous?"

She flashed a grin, but then it fell away. "Did you marry him so that he wouldn't lose his job?"

"You can't tell Beau."

"I won't bring it up, but if he asks, I'm not going to keep secrets. We've had issues with that." Lilith grabbed my hand. "There aren't many people Beau would jump in front of a bus to save, but you are one of those people. He cares about you, so it doesn't matter if he knows."

I filled another mug and slid it toward her. "I volunteered to marry Mad Dog to help him keep his job. He suggested that we sleep on it, and the next morning he showed up with flowers and gave me a ring. I was shocked that he proposed. But happy."

"What did he say when you left the house so early?"

"Nothing. He was still asleep."

"You managed to get out of bed and get clothes on without waking him?"

There was no point in holding back secrets now. "He slept in the guest room."

"What? Ava! That poor man. You made him sleep in the

guest room?" Lilith sipped her coffee then added more cream. "You need to go. If any of the ranch hands see you here, they'll rib Mad Dog. Don't do that to him."

I pointed at the stove. "When the oven is hot, put the pans in for forty-five minutes."

"You aren't upset with me, are you?" She lifted her eyebrows.

I shook my head. "I'm not." After hanging my apron back on the hook, I picked up my purse. "Our relationship isn't like what you have with Beau. Mad Dog and I don't sit around kissing and cuddling. We're friends."

Lilith hugged me. "You could see the attraction Beau and I shared even before we were willing to admit it. You saw how much your brother felt for Joji. What you can't see is how someone could feel that way about you."

I pinched the skin in that tender spot on my hand. "I should go."

"Ava, wait."

"What?" I gave her the courtesy of looking at her.

She smiled, and instead of pity, there was kindness in her eyes. "Have you talked to Mad Dog about what he wants?"

"He married me so he wouldn't lose his job." I smoothed my t-shirt. "I'm sure he doesn't want—"

"But have you asked him?"

"I know what the answer will be, and I'm not going to make him say it." Feeling raw and exposed, I walked out, needing time by myself.

Instead of going home, I drove out to where I used to cross the river. Without the bridge, I'd need a boat to get across. Because of the sharp rocks, I never swam in this part of the river.

Today I missed my little shack. It probably wasn't even safe to go inside the place after all these years.

Sitting on the tailgate, I listened to the rippling of the

water. Last night had set my mind at ease about how life would be, but Lilith's reaction had me questioning everything again.

The sun hadn't yet crested the horizon, and I'd probably get a lecture if the guys found out I was sitting out here before sunrise. But with Mad Dog at the house, I needed a place to think.

The situation wasn't really different than when I talked to Mad Dog at church or other gatherings. Now, we just talked at home. With that mindset, I could get through these first few weeks. After that, I expected my new life to feel normal.

I drove back to the house and quietly slipped inside.

"You're back." Mad Dog pointed over his shoulder toward the counter. "I just brewed a pot of coffee. Want a cup?"

"Please."

He filled a mug. "What do you take in your coffee?"

"A splash of cream and two cubes of sugar. I almost always have sugar cubes on hand. I like to feed them to the horses when I go out to the barn."

He prepped my coffee, then handed it to me. "How are you this morning?"

"I'm good. The weather is really nice. Later, I'm sure it will be hot as blazes."

He stared into his coffee cup. What was he thinking? I hated when he was so quiet.

Since he wasn't going to talk, I guess I had to. "Do you have plans with Poppy today?"

He shook his head. "She's spending the day with Cami."

Maybe he had expected me not to work today . . . and to spend the day with him. "Let me make you breakfast. What would you like?"

"I'm fine. I had cake." He picked up his coffee.

"Oh. Are you sure that's enough? I don't mind cooking for you. I have time. Lilith wouldn't even let me make breakfast this morning. I have a few bathrooms to clean because letting those go too long only makes the job harder."

He leaned against the counter next to me. "Are we still on for dinner?"

"Yes." I was looking forward to dinner. It felt like almost like a real date. But I didn't tell Mad Dog that. I knew he was trying to be nice because I was helping him.

He carried his coffee down the hall. "I have a few errands to run, but I'll be back in a couple of hours."

"All right. I'll probably be up at the main house."

Nodding, he closed himself in the guest room.

I served myself a giant piece of chocolate cake. More insulation was required.

CHAPTER 16

MAD DOG

*E*rrands were just an excuse to get out of the house. When Ava started talking about the weather, it felt like we'd taken a giant step backward. If I'd hung around, she would've been talking about pie in no time.

Instead of doing one of the many tasks awaiting me, I called my friend. "Jeff, you free?"

"I have time to shoot a few hoops."

"I'm on my way."

I'd known Jeffrey for many years. He'd lived not too far from my grandparents' ranch, and the two of us spent lots of hours hanging out together during the summers. Often, I was the one trying to keep him out of trouble, but I appreciated his friendship.

We'd kept in touch over the years, and now that we lived in the same town, we'd picked up where we'd left off. The best thing about Jeff was that he'd tell me when I was being an idiot.

I pulled through the gate and parked in front of his house. His spread wasn't anywhere as big as what Beau had, but

Jeffrey owned a herd of cattle. The place qualified as a working ranch.

He waved as I walked around to the side of the house, then tossed me the basketball. "That bad, huh?"

"What's bad? I had some time and thought a visit with my friend would be nice." I took the shot and missed.

Dribbling, he shook his head. "Lying is bad. You got married last night, and you are here playing basketball with me. I'm not great with relationships, but to me, that's bad. Plus, you never talk like that . . . a visit with my friend would be nice."

"Ava has toilets to clean."

"Ouch. Sorry." He did a layup, then passed me the ball.

My grand plan didn't seem possible. The lack of sleep probably attributed to that, but so did the mention of weather.

"Explain to me again why you married someone you haven't even dated? I know you've been working up to asking her out, but marriage first seems a bit extreme."

I launched the ball into the air, and it hit the rim and bounced off. "I've been out of the game too long. Why didn't I just ask her out months ago?"

"Because every time you tried, she talked about pie."

"Right. But I'm afraid that if I'm honest with her now, she'll think I'm trying to change the nature of the relationship."

He laughed. "Change the nature of the relationship. Funny. You put that very diplomatically."

"I'm serious."

"They say honesty is the best policy. Tell her that you think about her all the time, and that you've wanted to ask her out for months, but you were chicken. Then add a few things about how beautiful you think she is. Women love hearing that stuff, right?"

"I think that might be like a downpour in the desert. It'd do more harm than good." I stole the ball and finally landed it in the basket. "I think what she needs is more of a steady rain."

"Then you've answered your own question." He took another shot. "The way I see it is like this. You got this amazing cake, but you can't have any yet. You have to work your way through the dinner courses. And the first course is a first date. Ask the woman out."

"Do you even look at your reservations?" I dribbled around him, then lobbed the ball into the air. "We'll be dining at your table tonight."

He caught the ball and tucked it under his arm. "Good. And as much as I'd love to continue our fun little exchange, I need to get to work or there won't be any food tonight."

After a quick handshake, I climbed back into my truck.

It had been so long since I'd been on a first date. Before driving away, I searched up ideas to make the date special.

I'd already given Ava flowers and jewelry, so I wanted to figure out something else to give her. Peeps were a possibility, but I wanted to give her something that signaled my interest and not just that I listened to her.

Wine. I'd get us another bottle of wine. It would be a great opener to telling her how much I enjoyed talking with her and her giggles. Maybe I wouldn't mention the giggles yet.

Now I had errands to run.

HER TRUCK WASN'T at the house when I arrived. After stashing the gift and the Peeps—because having her favorite candy on hand seemed like a wise move when wooing—I set out for the main house.

The best way to grow our relationship was to spend time

together. And today, that meant cleaning toilets. With a pair of rubber gloves shoved in my pocket, I knocked.

Ava pulled open the door. "Oh, hi. I'm not quite done. I have two bathrooms left. The ranch hands' cabins took longer than I expected. I'm sorry."

"It's fine." I yanked the gloves out of my pocket. "I'm here to help."

She blinked. "Clean bathrooms?"

"Sure. There's no rule that says we have to be on the sofa drinking wine when we spend time together."

Her cheeks flushed. "Okay." She walked down the hall and into a bathroom. A bucket with cleaning supplies sat on the floor. "I planned to start by cleaning the tub."

"I'll scrub the toilet." I pulled out what I needed from the bucket. "What do you like to do for fun? Something just for you."

"I already told you about the cabin, but I haven't been there in years."

"Anything else?" I squirted blue liquid into the toilet bowl, then picked up the brush.

"You can't repeat this." She pushed a stray hair out of her face. "Promise?"

"I won't say a word."

"Belly dancing. There is a class that meets online. I don't make it every week, but it's so fun."

That was not the answer I'd expected. It was not even close to the range of what I expected, and I loved it. "Awesome."

I continued scrubbing, hoping that one day I might be invited to watch her dance.

When both bathrooms sparkled, we cleaned up and then headed into the dining hall.

"I'm making something easy for lunch today—grilled

cheese sandwiches. Would you mind grabbing a handful of those apples and cutting them up?"

"I can do that." I found a knife, bowl, and cutting board, then set to work. "I've enjoyed this. I can't do this every day because of my job, but if you don't mind me around, I might do this again."

"I don't mind at all." She laid out slices of bread on the griddle. "I'm looking forward to tonight."

That was exactly what I needed to hear.

"Me too. I got us a reservation at the restaurant across the road."

"I was surprised when I found out you knew the chef."

"He's a good friend."

"And a great cook." Ava smiled, and my hope returned.

Tonight would be a great first date.

CHAPTER 17

I stared at the bodysuit I'd bought the day I met Verbena. All the advice said that dressing pretty underneath would help me feel beautiful on the outside. I wasn't sure it would work, but what could it hurt to give it a try?

My blue dress wasn't too fitted, so I traded my shapewear for the sheer bodysuit. It wasn't as if anyone would see it, but maybe it would help me feel more attractive.

Now I just had to figure out how to get it on.

Was I supposed to wear a bra on top of it or under it? Skipping the bra wasn't an option because the sheer fabric couldn't hold anything anywhere.

Contorting my body, I managed to fasten the snaps between my legs. Why was I bothering with this? No one would see it.

And if I could successfully avoid glancing in the mirror, I wouldn't see it either.

I slipped into my blue dress and wrangled the zipper up. Then I looked in the mirror. I didn't look horrible. I'd never look like the models on the runway or the mannequins in the store—realistically, no one looked like the mannequins—but Mad Dog probably wouldn't run screaming.

I stepped into my heels, then opened the bedroom door.

Mad Dog leaned against the wall at the end of the hall with his arms crossed. "You look amazing."

What would he say if he knew what I was wearing under the dress?

"Thank you." I was far from used to his compliments, but at least now I wasn't fighting the urge to run away.

He held out a gift bag. "I got you a little something."

"You didn't have to do that." I strolled toward him, getting used to the heels I hadn't worn since forever.

"Something for you to remember our first date."

First date? We really were doing this all backward. I reined in my emotions. Now that we were married, he was making the best of the situation. Going out to dinner was a sweet gesture.

I lifted the tissue out of the top of the bag and smiled as I pulled out the frilly, flowery apron.

"Since you are magic in the kitchen, I thought of you when I saw that. And I picked up another bottle of wine . . . for when we feel like talking late into the night."

Holding the apron up in front of me, I blinked away happy tears. "I love it."

"Good." He held out his arm. "Shall we go?"

I looped my arm around his.

When we walked up to his truck, he opened my door.

As I stepped up, I felt a snap give way. Had it made a noise? Had he heard the snap pop free? I silently pleaded with the other two snaps to stay together until I could make it to the ladies' room at the restaurant.

Of course this would happen to me.

I barely let myself breathe, fearing that one deep breath would pop the other snaps right off.

Completely distracted, I stayed silent all the way to the restaurant.

My attempt to feel pretty didn't work because now I felt huge . . . too huge for pretty lingerie.

But I only had to make it through dinner.

The drive was short, and when he parked, I didn't wait for him to come around and help me out. I slid out, yanking on the end of my skirt, and praying I didn't flash him.

He clasped my hand as we walked toward the restaurant, and I was happy we were side by side.

The hostess greeted us when we walked inside and then led us to a table. It was in an alcove, separated from the other tables. The lights were dimmed, and candles flickered on the table. The whole scene was out of a romance movie, but I couldn't fully enjoy it because I was thinking about the stupid plastic snaps.

"Excuse me, where's the ladies' room?" I hoped it wasn't far from our table.

The hostess pointed to the opposite end of the dining room. "It's the first door on the right down that little hallway."

"Thank you." I smiled at Mad Dog, hoping he wouldn't pick up on my horror. "I'll be right back."

"Everything okay?"

"Yep." Lying again. I should never have married a pastor.

Waddling to the restroom would only draw unwanted attention, but walking normally risked working another snap free. I had to take the risk. Feeling like everyone in the room could see right through my dress, I kept my gaze fixed on the hallway. I locked myself into a stall and reattached the snap. I squeezed it together with a little extra oomph, hoping it would fuse the plastic together.

If the snaps got stuck, I could cut the bodysuit off me when I got home.

With my undergarments refastened, I strolled back to the table with a smile plastered on my face.

Mad Dog jumped up. His chivalry flattered me.

Easing into my chair, I sucked in a breath when a snap popped apart. If I went back to the bathroom now, he'd assume I was sick. As I slowly exhaled, I felt the other two snaps give way.

So much for feeling attractive. Now I just felt exposed.

"After dinner, if you'd like we could take a drive in the Hill Country."

Mad Dog's suggestion crashed through my panicked thoughts.

No way I was going to tell him the reason I wanted to dash home. "Maybe. We'll see how I feel after dinner."

"All right." He sounded disappointed.

I scanned the menu. "Everything sounds so good."

Our waiter walked up to the table. "What can I get you to drink?"

Mad Dog nodded at me to order first.

"Just water for me."

"I'll have tea." Mad Dog grinned as the Cowboy Chef walked up to the table.

"Evening. Thanks for coming in tonight." Jeffrey smiled. "Congratulations. Again."

"Thanks. Again." Mad Dog winked at me.

After a bit of small talk, the chef told us the specials.

We gave him our orders, and he sauntered back to the kitchen. The way Joji talked about the chef, it kind of surprised me that he was friends with Mad Dog.

"How do you know Jeffrey?" I tried not to think about the open snaps.

Mad Dog trailed a finger through the condensation on the side of his glass. "We met years ago when I spent my first summer with my grandparents. Every summer after that,

Jeffrey and I hung out. Now that I live here, I get together with him fairly often."

"I wouldn't have guessed you were friends. You're so different."

"He's got a little extra swagger, but deep inside, he's a great guy." Mad Dog leaned forward. "I've been thinking about places we could go. I know the summer is a busy time on the ranch. What if we planned a trip to the mountains in early fall? Would you like that?"

As naïve as the assumption might have been, I hadn't expected life to change much after marrying Mad Dog, but here he was talking about going on a vacation.

I probably looked foolish with my mouth hanging open while I tried to think of how to answer. "I didn't tell you about never leaving Texas just so you'd take me somewhere."

"I know. But if I planned a trip, would you go with me?"

"Yes."

We chatted until dinner arrived, and conversation never lulled or felt halted. Enjoying myself, I almost forgot about my clothing malfunction. Almost.

After dinner as we walked out of the restaurant, I reminded myself repeatedly that no one could see through my dress. That helped me make it through the room at a normal pace.

When we stepped outside, I touched Mad Dog's arm. "Would you mind if we stopped by the house before going to a drive? I'd like to change." More accurately, I wanted to put on some big old granny panties.

He brushed his hand against mine. "Wouldn't mind at all."

Neither of us moved. His hand felt warm against mine. As he hooked his pinkie around mine, he inched closer. The parking lot lights reflected in his brown eyes, and the gleam left me breathless.

Was he going to kiss me here in the middle of the parking lot?

The wind gusted, and my dress flipped up. I was horrified, imagining the other bits of sheer fabric whipping in the breeze. Mad Dog reacted quickly, and the only thing keeping me from embarrassment was his hand on my backside, holding my dress down.

I tensed.

When the wind stopped, he pulled his hand away. "Sorry. I was just trying to . . ."

Instead of wallowing in embarrassment, I pushed aside those emotions, choosing to focus on the developing friendship. "I'm not sure that's allowed on a first date." Grinning, I bumped his shoulder. "But thanks for the quick reaction."

He laughed. "I promise to keep my hands to myself on our drive."

I guess that answered the question about whether he was going to kiss me.

Climbing into the truck, I kept my dress tucked around my legs. "Mad Dog, I enjoyed myself tonight."

Leaning in close, he smiled. "I'm really happy to hear that. Any chance you'd go out with me again?"

I nodded. It wasn't like I would tell him no. We were married. But I couldn't wait until our second date.

He was working to make the best of a decision he'd made in haste. I could appreciate that. I just hoped he wouldn't regret his choice a few months down the road.

But the next time we went on a date, I wouldn't wear anything with snaps.

CHAPTER 18

MAD DOG

*A*nticipating that Ava would be up before the sun, I made sure we didn't stay out until all hours.

That decision proved to be a wise one.

When I heard her bedroom open, I sprang out of bed and yanked on a pair of jeans.

I headed straight for the coffee pot. "Morning."

Her cheeks flushed, but she smiled. "Hi. I can make that for you."

"I've been making my own coffee for ten years. I can do this. When are you leaving for the main house?"

"I usually have a cup of coffee, then eat something small before I head over. Cooking on an empty stomach makes me grumpy."

"Thanks for the warning."

Soft laughter filled the kitchen.

That alone was enough reward for being out of bed this early.

She touched my arm, then pulled her hand away. "I was going to scramble eggs. Want some?"

"Please." I pulled mugs out of the cabinet and fixed her coffee just how she liked it.

She glanced over her shoulder at me, but she wasn't looking at my face. "I'm surprised you're up this early."

I set a mug on the counter next to her and kissed her cheek. "You and me both. Mind if I tag along to breakfast?"

"You're always welcome to come." She lifted two plates out of the cabinet. "I had fun last night. Dinner and the drive."

"I did too. You free next weekend?"

"I'll put in a few extra hours this week to clear my weekend. After last week, I'm sure there are massive amounts of laundry waiting for me."

We sat at the table. I would live in a constant state of exhaustion by getting up with her every morning, but if our mornings were all like this, I could get used to this new normal.

I downed my coffee, then refilled the cup. "Have you considered Beau's offer to hire another person? Someone to clean."

"I should."

"Think about it." I poured the second cup of coffee down my throat, hoping the caffeine would kick in soon.

Once we finished breakfast, I cleared the table. "I'll get this cleaned up and meet you at the main house in a bit."

"Thanks." In a bold move for my bride, she hugged me. "Don't forget to put on a shirt."

Before I could think of something clever to say in response, she picked up her keys and walked out the door.

That hug was one more good thing about getting up early.

After cleaning the kitchen and taking a quick shower, I walked to the main house. Instead of shorts and tennis shoes,

I opted for jeans and boots. That was the required uniform on a ranch.

The room was full of ranch hands when I arrived. Some were seated at the table, already eating; others were at the counter, getting food.

Ava waved me over. "I set some bacon aside for you. I didn't want the boys to eat it all before you got here." She nodded toward the table. "Mason could probably eat half of it on his own."

"I don't doubt that. And thank you." I picked up the plate and loaded it with pancakes. "You made all this after leaving the house?"

"It doesn't take that long." She turned back to the griddle and flipped over the second round of pancakes. "Want more coffee?"

"I'll get it." I filled a mug and carried my plate to the table.

The guys were discussing plans for the day while Mason stuffed his mouth full of pancakes. He grinned and waved.

Clint dealt out assignments. "Archer had to fly home for a family emergency, so we are down one today. Working the calves will have to wait another day or two."

I made a snap decision. "If you need an extra set of hands, I'm happy to help."

Clint stared at me from the other end of the table. When Joji patted his arm, the effect was immediately evident. He relaxed his shoulders. "Thanks. I could use some help."

Ava sat down next to me. "Are you sure? What about Poppy?"

Mason's face lit up. "She's gonna swim with me."

I shrugged. "She said she would be busy until later. Now I know why." I ran a hand down Ava's arm. "We'd love for you to join us. Poppy said she'd text me later."

"Let me know." Ava leaned closer. "You don't have to work on the ranch."

"He won't hurt me, will he?" I didn't exactly whisper.

Clint chuckled from the other end of the table, and Joji nearly spit her coffee.

Ava rolled her eyes. "If he does, don't come running to me." Her words said one thing, but the gleam in her eye conveyed something completely different.

Progress.

IF IT WEREN'T for the country music playing on the radio, the truck would've been silent the whole way to the pasture.

When Clint shifted into park, he stared out through the windshield. "Did you volunteer so that you could talk to me about something?"

The look on his face strongly suggested that the right answer to that question wasn't yes.

"Nope."

"Try not to hurt yourself because Ava would hate me if something happened to you." He swung open his door and stepped out.

His matter-of-fact statement bounced around in my head. These little snippets of Ava through others' eyes gave me hope that deep inside her safety shell, she cared about me enough to let me love her.

I followed him through the pasture, scanning the livestock. "It's been a while since I've worked on a ranch, but I'll do my best to stay alive." At the end of the day, I'd regret not having a hat. Finding my old one was now on my to-do list for the week.

He stopped and slowly turned. "You worked on a ranch? Before or after you became a minister?"

"Before. My grandparents had a few hundred acres not

far from here, and I used to spend all my summers working on their ranch."

"Hmmm. The private investigator must've missed that." He pointed at the field of cows. "You worked the calves before?"

I nodded, still thinking about his last comment. "Wait. You ran a check on me?"

"Well, yeah. I hired Beau's son. You wanted to marry my sister." He opened the gate.

"Does she know?"

He yanked on his gloves. "Of course not."

I was careful not to promise that I wouldn't tell. Keeping secrets never ended well.

"But I'll warn you. It's been a while since I've done this."

He tossed me a pair of gloves. "Thanks for helping."

CONVERSATION DIED as we gathered the calves together. Clint barked orders, and I followed them. It took a while, but we managed to get the calves worked and tagged.

As I climbed into the truck, Clint tapped away on his phone. I expected that the ride back would be as quiet as the ride out.

Halfway back to the main house, Clint turned down the radio. "I didn't think my sister would ever marry." He shrugged. "But for that matter, I never thought I'd marry again. My point is . . . your marriage was a surprise. I'm not sure what to make of it, but as long as you treat her right, I'm okay with it."

"You didn't say any of this before."

"I guess I figured a minister would be good to her. And I wasn't going to do anything to discourage her. I want her to be happy. She deserves that."

"Clint, you have my word that I will love her." This conversation was worth the back-breaking hours of work.

"Until your dying day." He said it as a statement and not a question.

I understood the implication. "Absolutely."

He parked outside Ava's house. "Does she know that?"

"I'm working on it."

"Good." He nodded. "You were a big help. Thanks."

"Anytime." I climbed out and smiled as Ava stepped out onto the porch.

She met me at the top stair. "Clint messaged that you were on your way back. How was it?"

"I'm not as tough as I used to be, but we got the job done." If I hadn't been a complete mess, I would've pulled her close and kissed her.

But between the grime all over me and her brother sitting in a truck a few feet away, I opted for a kiss on the cheek.

She patted my chest. "You go shower. I'll warm your lunch."

After waving at Clint, I walked inside. I couldn't wait until Ava and I had another late-night, heart-to-heart conversation. Clint's comment about thinking she'd never marry had me wondering why. She'd opened up a little, but there was more to her story. And knowing it seemed important in gaining her trust.

"Thanks for coming home to meet me. It's kind of a treat to come home to someone." I undid the buttons on my shirt.

Pretending that she wasn't watching me, she wiped invisible crumbs off the table. "It is nice."

CHAPTER 19

*S*unday morning I woke up about as excited as a kid on the first day of summer school. Less than excited. I didn't want to go to church. But for Mad Dog, I would do it. He was worth it.

No one had said a word last Sunday, at least that Mad Dog had mentioned. I'd stayed home to work on wedding plans. And to avoid people.

I couldn't avoid anyone this week.

The drive to church seemed much longer than every other time I'd driven there. I continually reminded myself that I was helping Mad Dog, but I still dreaded the looks and whispers. Thanks to Lilith, I knew that word had spread about the lemon bar incident. Had the news of the wedding reached the congregation?

Maybe being here wasn't helping him at all. My presence had the potential to make everything worse. "I could've stayed home. I don't mind."

"Nonsense. I want you here." After parking in his reserved spot, he got out and ran around to my side, then held out his hand.

The warmth of his hand around mine calmed me, and I was glad he didn't let go.

"Would you like to sit in my office for a few minutes? I need to take care of a few things before the service starts."

I squeezed his hand. "People will talk if we close ourselves in your office. And there's been enough talk."

People could be vicious. And after years of blending in and not being interesting enough for anyone to gossip about, I was now in the spotlight. I didn't want to make it worse.

The corner of his mouth tugged into a smile as he pulled open one side of the double doors. "When people see the rings, I'm quite certain there will be more talk."

I nodded. "Yep. I'm afraid you're right."

We were almost to his office when Mrs. Beecham walked down the hall.

"Oh! I'm surprised to see you here, Pastor Miller." The woman didn't even look at me, let alone address me.

"Good morning." Mad Dog answered without any hint of snark.

I stopped outside his door. "I'll be in the sanctuary." I wanted to kiss him, but after what he'd said about not pretending, I didn't. But it took me half a second to decide that.

He stepped closer. "I'll meet you in there soon." Still holding my hand, he leaned down and softly brushed his lips on mine.

Blinking, I stared at him.

He rubbed my shoulder. "Save me a seat."

When Mrs. Beecham gasped, I grinned. Even if he was pretending, I didn't care. So worth it.

After a quick squeeze on his hand, I strolled toward the sanctuary like I belonged here.

While Mrs. Beecham stood gaping in the hallway, Mad Dog walked into his office and closed the door.

The gossip train had left the station.

In the sanctuary, I passed my favorite seat in the second row from the back. Since I was saving a seat for Mad Dog, sitting in the back wouldn't work. And pastors' wives probably weren't supposed to sit in the back of the church anyway.

The good thing about sitting in the front was that I wouldn't see all the people whispering.

Mad Dog usually sat in the first chair in the front row on the right side. Mrs. Beecham and her husband always sat in the second row right behind Mad Dog. Staring at the seats, I made a decision. And my motives were far from pure.

I sat on the left side and put my Bible in the seat next to me to save the seat for my husband. He wouldn't care where we sat.

But Mrs. Beecham would.

And Mr. Beecham was a creature of habit. Every Sunday, he showed up at the same time, greeted the same people, and sat in the same chair.

I checked the time, eager for people to come into the sanctuary.

After a few minutes, the doors opened at the back. It was too early for Mr. Beecham. He wouldn't enter for another two minutes.

A quick glance toward the back had my heart thumping. Mad Dog was greeting people as he walked to the front. Lots of people had arrived, and I hadn't even noticed.

Moments later, he picked up my Bible and sat down. Draping his arm across the back of my chair, he whispered, "Shaking things up, are we?"

I could feel heat flooding my cheeks. "Are we talking about getting married or the seats I chose?"

His breath tickled my ear. "Here they come. Let's see what happens."

Mr. Beecham shuffled up the aisle and dropped into his chair. Mrs. Beecham stopped before sitting down next to him. She looked at Mad Dog and then at the empty chair he typically occupied.

The only way I managed to observe the scene without being obvious was by looking at Mad Dog and quietly talking to him. My whispers were actually a play by play of what was happening.

When had I become so petty?

Mad Dog squeezed my shoulder as Mr. Beecham grumped. "Why are we moving? We never sit over here."

"Shh. Be quiet." Mrs. Beecham wasn't any nicer to her husband than she was to the rest of us.

The piano player started playing, and the music minister stepped up to the podium.

I'd made it this far, and it hadn't been too bad. Singing and listening to the sermon would be easy. Making it through the greeting time was another story.

Mad Dog opened the hymnal and put his arm around me so that we were close enough to share. I'd watched couples do this for years. Never did I think I'd be sharing a hymnal with anyone, let alone the pastor.

He sang out. His voice was deep and strong, and he hit every note perfectly.

I mumbled the words so he wouldn't be horrified by my inability to carry a tune.

In every way, I'd gotten the better end of this marriage deal. And it didn't seem fair to Mad Dog.

After three songs and a prayer, Mad Dog patted my leg as he stood, then walked to the front. He looked so handsome in his suit.

I'd always thought so, but after marrying him, I thought so even more. He seemed more handsome all the time.

I tried to listen to the sermon, but Mrs. Beecham whis-

pered through the whole service about how shocking it was
that the pastor had married me. While I didn't disagree, the
words were hard to hear.

As Mad Dog neared the end of his sermon, I considered
slipping out to the truck during the closing prayer. But I
didn't.

While he prayed, I pleaded with God to give me the grace
to smile at the people who'd whispered about me all through
the service.

Just as Mad Dog said "Amen," a hand touched mine.

Tessa, the talented woman who'd made my wedding cake
smiled. "I just wanted to tell you congratulations. You both
look so happy. But Cami is a little disappointed that she
didn't play a part in getting y'all together."

Tessa's friendly smile warmed my heart. "Thank you. I am
happy. And apologize to Cami for me. I'll have to see about
sending other people in need of matchmaking her way."

She laughed. "Cami would love that." After a quick hug,
she slipped away.

People stood and started heading for the doors, but
Reverend Saunders waved his hands and asked for everyone's attention.

Based on Mad Dog's expression, whatever announcement
the man intended to make was not expected.

"If I could have one moment. Please congratulate Pastor
Miller and his new bride, Ava. I had the pleasure of
marrying them just a few days ago." He clapped Mad Dog on
the back.

It would've been easier if news had spread through
gossip.

Mad Dog met my gaze and opened his hand. I took my
place at his side, smiling as people gathered around us, giving
congratulations.

Mr. Beecham flashed a grin as he stepped up. "Better

watch out, pastor. First she's changing where you sit. Who knows what she'll do next?"

Mad Dog slipped an arm around my waist. "I'm not too worried. A little change is good for everyone."

"I'm not sure about that." Mr. Beecham shook his head as he moved out of the way to let his wife have her turn.

She inhaled before speaking, and I leaned closer to Mad Dog, determined not to behave badly.

"I'm shocked." She propped her fists on her hips. "Completely shocked. And hurt that I wasn't invited." In a huff, she marched away.

Good thing she walked away because I had no response to that.

There were several others waiting for a turn, and while a few acted shocked, most seemed genuinely happy for us.

After the last person gave their congratulations, I checked the time. I always left an easy lunch for the guys on Sundays when I attended church, but I would need to prep dinner.

"I'm going to talk to Reverend Saunders for a minute." Mad Dog squeezed my hand. "You okay?"

Nodding, I smiled. "I'll meet you by your office."

I pushed open the doors and walked partway down the hall. The building had emptied out, and only a few people were still standing around talking.

"Excuse me, I don't mean to bother you." A woman who always sat at the other end of my favorite row in the back chewed her bottom lip.

"Not at all. It's Goldie, right?"

"Yes." She glanced down the hall and lowered her voice. "I just wanted to say how happy I was for you. I've been watching y'all for a while, wondering. And I think it's awesome that you married him. He's obviously smitten."

None of what she said made sense to me. My brain couldn't gather any words into a coherent sentence.

"And it gives me hope." She wiggled her empty ring finger. "Maybe my knight in shining armor is out there somewhere."

I needed to introduce Goldie to Cami.

Clutching Goldie's hand, I said, "I'm sure he is."

She glanced over my shoulder, then squeezed my hand. "See you next Sunday."

"Yes. It was nice talking to you."

She waved and walked out the door.

Mad Dog rubbed my back as he eased up beside me. "Are you ready?"

"As ever."

"Was it bad?"

I shook my head as I marched out of the building.

He didn't say anything else until we were in the truck. "If someone was rude to you—"

I touched his arm. "No one said anything horrible *to* me. But I hope you never feel trapped by your choice."

"I don't, and I won't." He clasped my hand. "Please believe that."

"I'm trying." I was learning to be honest with him little by little.

CHAPTER 20

MAD DOG

*O*ne month after the wedding, things were very much the same. I rolled out of bed before the sun to have coffee with Ava before she hurried to the main house to make breakfast for everyone.

Most mornings, I joined the ranch crew for breakfast before going to my office. I still hadn't gotten a lock for the door. On days I didn't work at the church, I helped out on the ranch. I'd forgotten how much I loved doing that.

Today I was at the church. I answered emails, trying to wrap up a few things before going to visit a couple of the older attendees who hadn't been able to attend services the last few weeks.

Reverend Saunders walked in, a doughnut in one hand and a huge smile on his face. "Good morning."

He'd officially retired weeks ago, but that didn't stop him from showing up at church almost daily. And the church secretary, who coordinated access to the building, hadn't asked for the church key back.

As a result, I was treated to surprise visits often.

"Morning, Reverend Saunders. How are you today?"

"Better now that I found that little bakery. Her stuff is good." He dropped into a chair. "And please call me Gary. How's married life?"

"Fine."

He stared out the window, bobbing his head. "I miss it. It's hard to go back to being alone after years of sharing your life." His gaze snapped to mine. "But you know all about that."

"I do. And it is nice to have someone to go home to."

The reverend's eyes twinkled. "And Ava's a good cook, I bet."

"She's a fabulous cook." It wasn't hard to tell that Reverend Saunders—Gary—wanted to be invited to dinner, but I'd have to check with Ava first. With her schedule, it wasn't exactly easy to have people over for dinner.

"Figured. You seem happier and"—he tapped his stomach —"well fed." Laughing, he stood and strolled toward the door.

"Have a nice day."

He waved before closing the door behind him.

What a wonderful start to my day. My extra pounds were noticeable. Ava's cooking was amazing, and when she was uneasy or bothered, she baked. She'd been baking almost non-stop all month.

The ranch hands joked that she made pies when she was upset, but she hadn't baked any pies all month. And that was fine with me. I loved the cakes, cookies, and other desserts she'd made.

But for me, keeping off the weight was important. Too many extra pounds, and I didn't feel like myself. I'd have to eat less dessert and get back to working out.

I could only imagine what I'd weigh if I hadn't been helping out on the ranch.

Focusing on what needed to be done, I scribbled down

the addresses of the people I needed to visit, then left a note for the secretary, letting her know I'd be out for a few hours.

Visits always took longer than I planned, but it was well worth the time. After visiting with several church members, I closed myself in the office and spent an hour working on the sermon.

MY PHONE RANG as I walked out to my truck. "Hello, sweetheart. How are things in New York?"

"Busy as always. How are you?"

"Great. I'm just heading home."

"I was, um, thinking . . ." Poppy was rarely hesitant to speak her mind, so the halted intro interested me.

"Yes?"

"I know it's only been a month since the wedding, and that I might be—how should I put this—in the way. But I was hoping I could come for a quick visit in a couple of weeks. I hardly spent any time with Ava. I'd love to get to know her better."

"I'll talk to her. I can't imagine that would be a problem."

It would be a problem. Ava wouldn't want Poppy to know that I was sleeping in the guest room, and Ava's other bedroom had no bed in it.

"Thanks, Dad. I enjoyed visiting the ranch, and I'm excited about going back. Parker said he'd give me another riding lesson."

"Parker, huh?"

"Totally not interested in anything more than lessons. I promise." She laughed, but there was an edge of nervousness to it.

Someone else on the ranch, besides Ava, had Poppy itching to return.

"I'm sure Mason will be thrilled." I switched over to Bluetooth and ran by the old house before going back to the ranch.

"He's such a cute kid." Voices sounded in the background. "I need to run. We are putting the finishing touches on a big presentation, so it'll be a late night."

"Love you. I'll text you and let you know what Ava says." I ended the call and ran into the nearly empty house. It hadn't taken as long to pack up the house as I'd anticipated. There was still a little bit of stuff waiting to be packed up, and I'd get to it soon.

In the extra room, I picked up my bass guitar case and amp. I'd mentioned to Ava that I played, and after not touching my instrument for a month, I was missing it.

Hopefully, she wouldn't find my playing disturbing. That wasn't something we'd discussed before getting married.

Glancing at the time as I pulled onto the ranch, I wondered if I'd catch Ava at home. She stayed busy, and some days, if I didn't wake up early and have coffee with her, I only saw her at meals with everyone else. I'd already suggested she let Beau hire an extra person, but nagging her about it would only make us both grumpy.

Ava was humming in the kitchen when I stepped inside. "Hello, I'm trying a new recipe. Taste this." She held up a truffle.

Obediently, I opened my mouth, and she popped the little ball of goodness inside. "Wow. That's great."

"Good. I made dozens and dozens. Help yourself." She wiped her hands on her apron.

Skipping dessert would be nearly impossible. I would have to be more intentional about working out.

"I'm going to go for a quick run before dinner unless you need something." I moved away from the counter where rows and rows of the tasty dessert balls were lined up.

"I'm good. We're having tacos tonight." She went back to humming as she dipped another batch of truffles into the white chocolate coating.

If she kept this up, I'd have to start running everywhere I went.

In the bedroom I changed into running shorts and a t-shirt. And the whole time, I was thinking about my conversation with Poppy. I shouldn't wait to ask Ava.

After she learned that Poppy wanted to come visit, Ava might spend the evening making another hundred dozen of those tasty truffles.

She handed me a bottle of water as I walked into the kitchen. "You'll need water. It's warm out. Do you know your way around enough?"

"I'll be fine. What's the worst that can happen?"

Her head moved back and forth, and she waggled a finger at me. "Never ask that question."

"Noted." I popped another truffle in my mouth. "Poppy called me. She wanted to come for a visit."

"Oh, that's nice. When is she coming?"

"She said in a couple of weeks. Do you mind if she stays here since my house is almost empty?" I watched for her reaction to the question.

She opened her mouth, then closed it again. After half a second she looked at me. "I don't mind, but we'd have to . . ." Another tray of truffles got pulled out of the freezer. "That's fine. I'd love it if she stayed here."

"Ava, I can ask Beau about having her stay in one of the little cabins."

"No. She can stay here. I'd hate for her to think we didn't want her at our house."

I leaned against the counter. "I'll talk to Beau. Poppy won't think we don't want her here. She'll assume we're newlyweds who don't want other people in the house."

Ava pinched her lips together. "I feel like we're lying to everyone."

"Do you care about me?" I chose my words carefully.

Her brown eyes brimmed with tears. "I do."

"And I care deeply for you. How is that a lie?" I opened my arms.

She stepped into the embrace. "I'm not sorry we got married. And I think it would be good if she stayed here. You can stay in my room. Unless you don't want to."

Oh, I wanted to. "That sounds great to me. I'll let her know." After dropping a kiss on top of Ava's head, I pulled back. "With all the yummy things you make, I need to burn some calories. I'll be back."

She followed me to the door and watched as I jogged away from the house.

How could I convince Poppy to move to San Antonio and stay with us for the first few months?

Thinking about Poppy's visit, I had forgotten to ask Ava about having Reverend Saunders over for dinner. Probably for the best. I didn't want to overload Ava all at once.

CHAPTER 21

AVA

Typically, I only served dessert on the weekends. Since getting married, I'd provided dessert options every night. Those who knew me well would think something was wrong. But I couldn't help myself.

While the taco meat cooked, I mixed cake batter. I cared about Mad Dog. I wanted his daughter to think of me as family. But the idea of sharing a bed with him terrified me. I didn't think he'd do anything horrible. He was much too kind a person, but I didn't want him to be disappointed.

For the last month, I'd baked because I knew he loved what I made. And I was doing my best to make him happy. It also calmed me. A win-win.

Lilith grinned as she walked into the dining room. "Baking again? Joji already added an extra goat yoga class every week. I'm going to have to swim laps before work if you keep this up."

"Mad Dog likes the stuff I make."

"We all do." She leaned on the counter. "Is that the only reason you're baking?"

I rolled my eyes and slid the pans into the oven. "You know it's not."

"Do you regret marrying him?"

"No!" Even with all my insecurities, I didn't regret my decision. "But I am afraid that one day he'll wake up and regret marrying me. Look at me, Lilith. No one was beating down my door." I shut up when I caught movement near the door.

"You're beautiful." Lilith clearly hadn't seen Mad Dog walk into the room.

His hair was still damp, presumably from a shower. He walked up and kissed my cheek. "See, I'm not the only who thinks so."

Lilith pointed outside. "Beau is on the back patio."

Mad Dog took the hint. "Call me when the food is ready."

I waited until he was clear of the door. "Why did you do that? He's going to think we're talking about him." I stirred the meat, then tasted it to make sure it was seasoned just right.

"We *are* talking about him." She tapped a perfectly manicured nail on the counter. "Have you considered the idea that maybe he has feelings for you? And do you know how ridiculous it sounds for me to be saying that about your husband?"

"Assuming he doesn't love me that way is easier. I swore I'd never marry. And I have reasons for that."

"But you *are* married. If nothing else, you need to talk to him about those reasons." She tapped the counter and backed away when Parker strolled into the room. "Think about it."

"Go let the guys know the food is ready." I waved her out of the room. "Hiya, Parker, how was your day?"

"Hot. Where do we put in the order for cooler weather?" He hung his hat near the door.

"Dearie, it's June. We won't get cooler weather for

months." I handed him a glass of tea. "Tell those horses to flap their tails faster to get you some air."

"Air from the back of the horse isn't always pleasant." He chuckled.

I tried not to have favorites. All the guys were dear to me, but Parker and Kent were special. And Mason had stolen my heart from day one.

I slipped a truffle to Parker. "What do you think of this? It's made with Oreos and cream cheese."

He moaned after biting into it. "Please tell me you have many more of these."

"Tons, but after tacos. And don't mention them in front of Mason until after he eats."

"Yes, ma'am." He nodded toward the door. "Your sweetie's here. Are you going to let him try one?"

"He's already had some." I retreated to safety behind the counter.

Mad Dog sat down across from Parker, and they talked as the other guys wandered into the room.

Maybe Lilith was right. It was probably time for another late-night chat.

I SET up my laptop and connected to the online belly-dancing class. I'd missed several classes since getting married because I never joined when Mad Dog was home. But this evening he was visiting someone in the hospital.

Every day on the ranch I wore basically the same thing: jeans, a t-shirt, and boots. For belly-dancing class I wore leggings, and no one but the people in this class ever saw me in leggings. Well, the ladies at goat yoga did. And the one time Clint came out and joined the class, all the guys looked on, but no one was watching me or even noticed what I was wearing. As a rule, it was best that my friends didn't see me in tight-fitting clothes. Having them running away screaming wasn't a great morale builder.

With all the blinds closed, I breathed in deep as the instructor started the class. After stretching, I tied on my hip scarf that had small silver coins attached. We walked through the basic steps, building muscle memory.

The best part of the class—at least it was my favorite—was when the instructor turned on one of her favorite songs, and we all danced. I turned up the volume, ready to lose myself in the music. With each song, I relaxed a bit more, enjoying the movement and the jingling of the coins.

Watching the screen, I kept my arms extended and shimmied. I'd practiced this move a lot. Whenever I was alone in the kitchen, I'd shake my hips, perfecting the repeated motion. And the jingle of my hip scarf made me happy.

The song ended, and I fanned myself.

"Need this?" Mad Dog stepped up beside me with a water bottle in his hand.

How had I not heard him come in?

I glanced down at what I was wearing. "You're here." That was an astute statement.

"And glad I am, but I'm going to head into the bedroom and let you finish your class." His gaze drifted downward. "I like your scarf."

There weren't near enough coins to hide the bulky hips underneath it.

The look on his face made me want to throw myself into his arms, but my embarrassment nixed that idea.

"Okay." I was full of wise things to say tonight.

Part of me was afraid Mad Dog would decide he'd made a mistake, and the longer we were married, the more my feelings for him grew. And if he left, it would leave a huge bruise on my heart.

But the other part of me was afraid that maybe he did feel something for me. The look in his eye just then fueled those thoughts. But I wasn't sure I could love him back, not in that way.

I could feed him and do his laundry. But what if he decided that wasn't enough?

CHAPTER 22

MAD DOG

I stayed in my room until Ava knocked on the door. She'd changed out of her belly-dancing clothes and into those flannel pajamas. I'd seen a lot of those flannel pajamas.

"I'm done with the class. Would you like a glass of wine?" She crossed her arms.

Wine meant conversation. "I'd love one. I can get it."

She stayed beside me as we walked to the kitchen. "I was thinking we could talk."

"Absolutely." I uncorked the wine and poured us each a glass.

Cradling hers, she sat down at one end of the couch. Reading her cues, I sat at the other end.

After trailing her finger along the rim of the glass for a second, she bit her bottom lip. "Is this what you were expecting when we talked about getting married? Because if it isn't, you don't have to stay. Blame it on me. You can say I didn't want to be married." She pulled her knees to her chest, almost cocooned.

"I'm not leaving, Ava."

She stuck her foot out, pressing her socked foot against my leg. "Really?"

I rubbed her foot. "For better or for worse. Till death do us part. I meant that."

"I see you going for your runs and doing your pullups and pushups, and I feel guilty that I don't work out enough."

"I run and work out because I enjoy it, and because too much added weight makes my body ache. I never meant it as a hint that you should be exercising. The thought never crossed my mind. Not to mention that you work harder than anyone else on the ranch."

"That's not true." She stared into her glass. "For as long as I remember, I haven't been thin. In high school, I didn't weigh as much as I do now, but I wasn't skinny. Big boned is how they described me back then. Some people at least. My father, before he left us, used to just call me fat."

"I'm sorry he spoke to you that way." I kept my voice calm even though I wanted to pound the man, wherever he was.

"I shouldn't care what he thought. He wasn't a good person, and I'm not sorry he left. But I'm not sure . . ." She sipped her wine.

I shifted her foot into my lap and scooted closer to her but stayed quiet.

"The idea of letting someone see me is horrifying, and I swore I'd never marry because of that and other things, but when all that happened with the . . . you know . . ."

"Lemon bars?"

She nodded. "You needed my help, but I didn't think you'd want . . ."

Silence hung in the air for several heartbeats.

"Why else didn't you want to get married?" The answer would make me mad, but the question had to be asked.

Staring at the ripples dancing across the top of her wine, she chewed her bottom lip. "My father was awful to my mom. Just horrible. He'd hit her when he was drunk, and not once did I ever hear him compliment her on anything. I wasn't going to risk ending up like that."

I rubbed her foot. "That's awful."

A small smile broke through the pain etched on her face. "I agreed to marry you because I knew you wouldn't hurt me. Not like that."

I had a better understanding of what this ranch meant to her and how much it meant for her to marry me. "You told me how this ranch was your safe place. And I've moved in and disrupted all that. I'm sorry." I continued to massage her foot. I wanted to be her safe place, and I hoped the slow and steady approach would convince her of that in time.

Timidly, she extended her other foot. "I like having you here."

Kneading her feet felt intimate. "I enjoyed our first date. And I'd love to go on a second one."

"About that. You could probably tell, but I've been extra busy."

"I know you're busy, and I don't want to be a demand on your time."

She rested a hand on mine. "I've been extra busy on purpose. I haven't dated in decades. Maybe longer than that. I'm completely out of my element. Put me in a kitchen, and I'm capable of anything. Give me a bucket of cleaning supplies, and I can do wonders."

"What we're doing here, talking and being honest, is how I picture dating. And I haven't dated since Marlene died."

"I'll talk to Beau tomorrow about hiring someone to clean and about getting extra help to cover meals on the weekends." She stared at my hands rubbing her feet. "Because I don't want to be too busy to spend time with you."

"Thank you. That means a lot."

"And I can't believe that I'm saying this, but since we're already married, I need to say it." Her lip quivered.

"Ava, I'm not asking you to do anything that makes you uncomfortable. Please know that." I meant every word even if it resulted in spending the rest of my married life in the guest room.

Tears glistened in her eyes as she smiled. "If I've learned anything from my brother this past year, it's that being uncomfortable isn't always a bad thing, and I know that you would never push me to do something I didn't want to do." She blinked away the tears. "What I'm trying to say is, if we take it slowly—and I'm talking getting passed by snails—I'm willing to explore a romantic relationship with you."

I swallowed the lump in my throat. Rarely was I rendered speechless, but how was I supposed to respond to getting such a tender and precious gift?

She pulled her feet back and pushed off the couch. "If you don't want that, I understand." After setting her nearly full wine glass on the coffee table, she darted toward her bedroom.

I caught up to her halfway down the hall. "I want that. My quiet was because I'm a little emotional." I held out my hand. "Why don't you come back to the couch and finish your wine?"

She stared at my hand for several heartbeats before slipping her fingers into my hand. "Okay."

When we sat down, she kept her hand in mine.

I handed her the glass. "Let me know when you have your classes, and I'll disappear until they're over. Not because I don't like the way you look in your leggings and hip scarf because saying that would be a lie, but because I want you to feel comfortable and be able to do what you enjoy." I sipped the last bit of my wine. "When I tell you that I think you're beautiful, I'm not lying to you or pretending for appearance's sake. I mean every word."

Pink crept up from below her collar, and the blush continued up to her face. Grinning, she drank her wine.

The image of that smile behind the rim of the glass would forever be etched in my memory.

She poked me in the leg. "Just so you know, it doesn't bother me when you walk around the house without a shirt on."

"And it won't bother me if you do it too."

Her laugh echoed off the walls.

I loved our late-night chats.

CHAPTER 23

*W*hile I prepped breakfast, I thought about the late-night chat. Being honest with Mad Dog had been easier than I'd expected. Having him rub my feet helped.

After making sure everything was set out and ready, I checked the timer. The breakfast casserole only needed another ten minutes. I had enough time to talk to Beau, and he was probably up by now. I peeked into the main part of the house. He was sitting in the kitchen nursing a cup of coffee.

"Morning. Have you finished at least one cup?" I knew better than to start business conversations with him before he'd had at least half a mug of coffee.

Chuckling, he tapped the stool next to him. "Mostly. What's up?"

"You've offered multiple times to hire someone to help me."

His eyebrows lifted in surprise. "Are you saying yes to my offer?"

"I am. Also, if possible, I'd like to have the weekends off." I was a tad nervous about his reaction to that request. No one else at the ranch took the weekends off.

He downed the rest of his coffee. "Mad Dog deserves a medal. I've been trying to get you to slow down for years. After one month, here you are." He walked to the coffee pot and poured himself another cup. "You can absolutely have the weekends off. I'll start posting ads today."

"Thanks, Beau." I slipped off the stool.

He caught my hand. "I'm really happy for you, Ava. Mad Dog is a lucky guy."

"I think you have it backward." I was the lucky one. "And I'll cover stuff until we find someone."

"I appreciate that, but until I find someone, I'll handle breakfast on Saturdays and Sundays."

I slapped a hand over my mouth too late to hold back my laugh. "Sorry, but, darlin', no one wants to eat what you cook."

"Cereal and milk. Or I'll run into town and get dough-nuts. We'll survive."

I hugged him. "I'm not going to argue. Thanks."

He patted my back. "You're family, Ava. And always will be."

My timer would be going off any moment. "I need to get breakfast out of the oven. The guys will be in to eat soon." I rushed back to the mess hall.

Mad Dog grinned from a spot at the table. There was a steaming cup of coffee in his hand. "There you are. I made a pot of coffee."

"Thanks." I poured it into a carafe and started the second pot. "I was in the house talking to Beau. He'll post ads to find extra help."

Mad Dog strolled up to the counter, never breaking eye contact. "Then as soon as weekends are covered, we'll go on that second date."

I inched closer. "I vote that we go out Friday night. I'll do something easy for the guys for dinner, and Beau insists that he's covering breakfast Saturday morning."

"I'm not expected to actually eat what he serves, right?" Humor glinted in Mad Dog's eyes.

I rested a hand on his chest. "I'll be your personal chef that morning."

That same look of desire danced in his eyes, but this time instead of running away, I leaned in close and pressed my lips to his.

When I pulled away, I stared at the buttons on his shirt half a second before meeting his gaze.

"You made my day." He winked. "I'm really looking forward to Friday night."

"Snails. Remember that."

"I'll see if I can find a place that serves escargot." Wearing a heart-melting grin, he leaned in close and kissed my cheek before whispering, "And clearly you are quite capable in the kitchen."

"You are going to have me bright red when the boys get here."

He laughed as footsteps sounded on the porch. "Is that a problem?"

I shoved on his chest. "Take your coffee and go sit."

"Yes, ma'am."

He sat facing the counter, and anytime I glanced his way —which was often—he smiled in a way that didn't seem appropriate for a minister at all.

Being married wasn't really so bad.

THAT EVENING, I wiped down the counter, waiting on the enchilada casserole to finish heating. The salad was ready, and beans were in the crockpot.

I hadn't seen Mad Dog since he'd left after breakfast. All day, I replayed the kiss in my head, proud of my courage and even more delighted with his reaction.

Mason looked up from his coloring book. "Do I have to eat salad? I don't like tomatoes."

"I have a bowl made especially for you. It doesn't have any tomatoes on it."

He grinned. "Thanks Miss Ava. Parker doesn't like tomatoes either."

"And I have a bowl for him too."

Whistling sounded outside, and my heart fluttered. Mad Dog was here. Part of me was still nervous, but more of me was eager to see him and excited to be close to him.

"Evening." He crossed the room and kissed my forehead. "How was your day?"

"Good. A little busy."

Mason ran over and tugged on Mad Dog's sleeve. "You aren't supposed to kiss her like that. Remember?"

Crinkles appeared near Mad Dog's eyes. "How could I forget?" He laced his fingers with mine. "Mason told me that Clint married Miss Joji because he liked kissing her on the lips."

Mason propped his hands on his hips. "Cause that's how married people are supposed to kiss."

I could feel my cheeks heating. "Who taught you that?"

He tossed his head back in exasperation. "*Everybody* knows that. Ask Mr. Clint."

Mad Dog bit his lip, clearly trying not to laugh. "Maybe you should ask him about it during dinner."

There was one way to end this conversation. I kissed Mad Dog. On the lips.

And when I did, Mad Dog pulled me closer, deepening the kiss. One hand moved to my cheek, and all my bones turned to jelly. After breaking the kiss, he whispered in my ear. "I think that's how married people kiss."

"Uh-huh." I dropped my head onto his shoulder. "I'm glad we're married."

"Me too." The gravelly rumble of his voice made my heart beat faster.

Mason strode back to the table, his boots clunking on the stained concrete floor. "Some kids at school kiss like they're married, but Mr. Clint told me I shouldn't kiss my friends that way."

Mad Dog's shoulders bounced, but he didn't make a sound.

I whispered in his ear. "Do not bring that up at dinner."

"Yes, ma'am."

Usually that phrase made me feel old, but the way Mad Dog said it made me feel something completely different.

"Oh, I forgot to mention, Reverend Saunders was hinting that he'd like an invitation to dinner. Any chance we could make that work one night? He's lonely. I know he'd appreciate it."

"See if he's free Saturday night. I'll make a meatloaf." I pulled the casserole out of the oven.

After making sure the oven was off, I turned back to face Mad Dog.

"Thank you. That's sweet. I have one more question." He inched closer.

"Hurry because everyone will be here in about a minute."

"What about dancing on Friday night?"

"Dancing?" The idea of an evening in his arms had every one of my nerves tingling.

He patted my arm. "Just think about it."

Between the kisses and our date and planning a meal for the reverend, I had lots to think about.

CHAPTER 24

*A*va let go of my hand as we walked off the dance floor and lifted her hair off her neck before letting it fall again. I hadn't missed the fact that she'd worn her hair down, which she hadn't done on our first date.

"Would you like something from the bar?" I leaned in close so she could hear me over the loud music.

After biting her lip, she nodded. "A margarita sounds good."

"Coming right up." I'd been careful not to hold her too close early in the evening. But trying to move at a snail's pace wasn't easy.

When I walked back to the table with two bottles of water and her margarita, she smiled. "This is so fun. I'm glad you suggested it. I love dancing, but I get to do it so rarely."

"Great. I suggested it because it seemed like a good excuse to hold you close through most of the evening." I set her drink on the table.

With the neon reflecting in her brown eyes, she rested a hand on my chest. "You don't need an excuse."

Since I couldn't think of anything to say, I pressed my lips to hers. Her hand slid up my chest and around my neck. As a crowd scooted around the floor to the rhythm of the bass guitar, our hearts thumped to the same beat.

After breaking away, she glanced at her drink before meeting my gaze again. "You know what else I rarely do?"

Quite sure that "kiss me like that" wasn't the answer she expected, I responded with a question instead. "What's that?"

"Drink when I'm not at home. And even there, I don't drink much, but you probably guessed that because after one glass of wine, I start giggling."

"And after two, you fall into my lap."

Her brow furrowed, and she poked at the ice with the tiny straw. "I was only planning to have one glass tonight."

I shifted behind her and slid my arms around her waist. "I'm not asking for more. Not tonight."

"I'm not sure when . . ." She leaned back against me.

"When you're ready, tell me. Until then, we'll dance." It was the frankest conversation about intimacy we'd ever had, and my answer hadn't sent her running.

Quite the opposite.

She tilted her face to look up at me. "And kiss."

"Absolutely. But probably not at the same time."

"I'd fall over for sure." She sipped her drink, then slid off the stool. "I like this song. I heard you playing this on the bass, didn't I?"

"You did. I like this song too. The lyrics are clever."

Even in the dimly lit dance hall, I could see the blush creeping up her cheeks.

"Not hard to figure out what he means, is it?" Tugging me toward the dance floor, she sang along as the band played Nothing on but the Radio.

We danced, and after several songs, there was no gap between us as we made our way around the floor.

After several hours of dancing and talking and people

watching, I led her off the dance floor. "Want another drink? A water or something?"

"I think I'm ready to head home." She laced her fingers with mine. "I'm sure Beau has everything needed to make margaritas. We could pick it up from the main house before going home."

"I like that idea."

"I'll text him and tell him to set it in the mess hall." She squeezed my hand as we stepped outside and left the roar of noise behind. "Have you ever been in a band?"

"A long time ago. But playing late on Saturday nights and preaching on Sunday mornings didn't work so well."

"Have you always been a pastor?"

I opened her door and helped her into the truck. "Beside the occasional odd job, yes. When I first started, I worked with youth. After a few years, I moved up to big people."

"Big people." She giggled. "I've been thinking about Reverend Saunders. What's his first name? Does he mind if I call him something else? Reverend sounds so stuffy."

"Gary. And I doubt he'd mind at all. But I'm curious about why you've been thinking of him."

"I've been thinking about what you said about him being lonely. Widowed and retired, he must not have much to do."

"He stops by the church fairly often."

She pressed on my chest. "Get in the truck. We'll talk while you drive."

I'd never get tired of her touching me. She'd done it much more this week, and this time she didn't seem the least bit tense when she did.

As I pulled out of the lot, she continued her thought. "Tessa is the lady at the bakery. She's friends with Cami. You remember Cami, right?"

"I do. She's not very forgettable."

"I wish I had a little more of her spunk. Anyway, Cami

likes to matchmake. I'm not sure if that's a real word or a made-up word. But she tried to help Clint realize his feelings for Joji. That's a whole other story, but . . . I am working my way to a point." She shook her head. "Sorry it's taking me so long."

"Don't apologize. I'm listening." I loved seeing her relaxed.

"Maybe we should set the reverend—I mean Gary—up with someone. I could ask Cami, or . . . oh! What about that nice lady I met shopping?"

"Verbena? That might not be a bad idea. I think tomorrow night is too soon though." No one would want to be put in an uncomfortable situation. "What if we hosted a gathering and invited both of them? Rather than just setting them up."

"You're a natural at this." She ran her hand down my arm and clasped my hand.

When I arrived at the main house, Ava squeezed my hand. "He said it would be on the counter. I'll wait here."

I leaned over and enjoyed a moment of kissing her like married people were supposed to do. "Be right back."

The mess hall was dark, but rather than turn on a light, I used my phone's flashlight. The stash of alcohol was easy to spot on the counter, and I made my way across the room.

Once I had the tequila, triple sec, and margarita mix in hand, I walked back toward the door.

"Have a good time." Beau chuckled from the doorway of the game room.

I somehow managed not to drop the bottles. "Thanks. Didn't meant to disturb you."

Lilith poked her head over Beau's shoulder. "You didn't. We were waiting. How are things?"

What a loaded question.

"Fine." With Ava in such a good mood, I wasn't going to linger here talking to them. "Night."

Our relationship was deepening. There was romance, but more importantly, there was trust.

When we got back to Ava's, I mixed us drinks and we snuggled on the couch and talked for over an hour. She shared more about the years growing up, and I told her more about the time I'd spent on my grandparents' ranch.

It was well past midnight when she stood up. "I'm about to fall asleep sitting up. As much as I love talking to you, I have to go to bed."

I started to stand up, but she shook her head.

"I had two drinks." She giggled as she eased into my lap.

"And I didn't even have to trip you this time."

Her lips pinched together. "I'm not crushing you, am I?"

"Not at all." I pulled her to my lips.

When I'd walked down the aisle, I'd chosen to love her. Now, I had all the flutters of a teenager with a crush. We really were doing this whole thing backward.

But I wasn't going to complain.

I LEANED against the wall and watched as Ava buzzed around the kitchen. Today had been nearly perfect. She'd slept in until well after the sun was up. We'd walked along the river and talked about visiting the mountains in the fall. And now she was in the kitchen, wearing the apron I gave her as she finished making dinner.

"Are you just going to stand there watching me?" She glanced over her shoulder.

"Unfortunately, I have to leave. I told Gary I'd meet him at the front gate. I didn't want him showing up to the wrong house or cabin." I pulled my keys out of my pocket. "But I like this view."

She didn't turn around, but I could see her cheeks lift in a smile. "You better hurry. We don't want him getting lost."

"How much trouble could he find?"

She shook her head. "Don't ask questions like that. It's never a good idea."

I walked away from the picture of domestic bliss to meet the reverend. By the time I had him back at the house, Ava had the table set, and the food was ready.

She smiled as we walked in the door. "Welcome. Come on in."

"I've been looking forward to this ever since Mad Dog invited me." Gary sniffed the air. "Smells good."

"Have a seat at the table. What can I get you to drink? We have sweet tea, sodas, coffee."

"Sweet tea would be good." He sat down looked around the kitchen. "Thank you for having me. I don't get many home-cooked meals anymore. Even the company is nice. If it weren't for Mad Dog, some days I might not get to talk to anyone."

Ava passed our drinks before taking a seat. "Why did you retire?"

Gary shrugged. "I'm sixty-five, and I was encouraged to enjoy the next phase of life. Phooey. It's lonely, and I don't like it."

"You could unretire or whatever the word for that is." My wheels were turning. I was loving my work on the ranch, and with someone else willing to preach, that could open up possibilities.

He chuckled. "Surely I can't be the only one who didn't take to retirement."

"Maybe you could—" Ava stopped mid-sentence.

I waited a second to see if she'd complete the thought, but she didn't. All I got was a glance and an apologetic smile.

I could guess what she hadn't said. "Gary, with the extra time on your hands—at least until you figure out what you want to do—maybe you could help me from time to time. In fact, Poppy is coming next weekend. Would you be willing to do the sermon on Sunday? That would give me more time to spend with her, and she's heard me preach plenty."

"Yes, of course." His smile widened. "I'm happy to help. And Ava, this meatloaf is delicious."

"Thank you." She beamed. "I think it's a great idea about you helping Mad Dog."

I pointed at the food. "This is the best meatloaf I've ever had."

She understood the significance of my statement, and her delight shown in her eyes.

Wanting to make me a food that I loved, she'd made something even better. Somehow that seemed like an allegory for our marriage. She married me to help me, but what I'd gotten was so much more.

We weren't acting married in every sense of the word, but I was definitely in love. More than that, I felt loved. Progress.

CHAPTER 25

Still half asleep, I knocked on the guest room door.
Mad Dog opened it and scrubbed his face.
"Morning. What's up?"

A question I'd wondered about but never asked was now answered. He slept in boxer briefs.

"I, um . . ." If I didn't quit staring at his chest, I'd never get the words out. "Lilith called. Last night's storm blew over a tree which knocked down a fence. Cattle are scattered. I'm going to throw together a quick and portable breakfast for the guys. Lilith has an event today, and Joji is getting ready to sell cheese at the weekend market." Surveying him once more, I blew out a breath. "I hated to wake you, but I . . ." Why had I woken him up? I could've sent him a text, letting him know.

He startled me with a quick kiss. "Thanks. Let me throw clothes on, and I can go help them. If it takes a while, do you mind getting Poppy?"

"Of course. I mean, I don't mind." I pointed at the door. "I'll meet you over there."

He nodded and closed the door.

Sleeping in on the weekends was a treat I was learning to love, but that view of Mad Dog was also a treat. Totally worth getting up before the sun.

The mess hall smelled of coffee. Lilith must've made a pot before heading over to the venue. I poured it into a carafe and made a second pot. These guys would need coffee this morning.

While bacon crumbles crisped up in a pan, I scrambled three dozen eggs in a separate pan. Once everything was cooked, I mixed it and wrapped up several dozen breakfast tacos. Portable, they were easy for the guys to eat on the run.

Mad Dog walked in just as I finished prepping everything. "Sorry it took me so long. I called Poppy to let her know."

"Here. Carry this box out to the truck. Coffee and disposable cups are in there. And I'll grab the tacos. I think most of the guys are out in the north pasture. But that wasn't the only fence that broke apparently."

We climbed into his truck and drove out to meet the guys.

Not only were they happy for food and coffee, but they seemed glad for the extra set of hands.

Clint patted Mad Dog's shoulder. "I didn't want to ask because I know Poppy is coming."

"Y'all need help. Besides, I'm fairly sure Poppy is more excited about spending time with Ava and Mason." Mad Dog set his old, tattered hat on his head.

"Where is Mason?" I looked around but didn't see him or Kent.

"I thought Kent was going to meet you in the mess hall." Clint glanced at his phone. "Oh. He missed you. Want him to come out here?"

"That works. Y'all eat." I handed out tacos and poured coffee.

Mad Dog handed me his keys. "You'll need these."

As he stepped away, I caught his arm. "Be careful."

"Always."

I inched up on my toes and pressed a kiss to his lips. "I mean it."

In only a short time, he'd become a part of my life I never wanted to be without. There was a word for the feelings I harbored toward Mad Dog, but I wasn't ready to use the L word. Mutual affection would have to suffice until I was a bit braver.

Grinning, he waved as he walked toward the field. And without apology, I watched him.

"Um, Ava, when you're done staring at your husband, can I get food and a coffee?" Parker bit his lip, but it didn't hide his smirk.

"Sure thing, dear. Give me just another second." I winked. "Here you go."

He wolfed down his taco in two bites, and I handed over another.

He ate the second a bit more slowly. "I think it's good that you found someone special. You're always taking care of all us guys. I hope he does a good job of taking care of you."

"He does."

Mad Dog mounted a horse and rode off with Beau. I would never have looked twice at Mad Dog if I'd met him when he was cowboying. Not because he didn't look good. Quite the opposite. This rugged version of him turned my heart into a one-man band, thumping and whizzing. But when I was younger, I steered clear of cowboys because most of them were gruff and tough. I knew some who weren't, but why bring logic into it?

Mad Dog had captured my attention because of his kindness.

Seeing that kindness wrapped up in that rugged package was more than I'd ever dared to dream.

"Ahem." Kent broke through my thought bubble.

Parker laughed. "See that dot in the distance? That's Mad Dog. She's watching him."

"I like Mad Dog. He's cool." Mason sounded like a little man.

"Me too." After tousling his hair, I handed out more food. "Mason dear, you are going to stay with me until they get the cows back together and the fences fixed."

"Fun! Maybe we can go swimming." He raised his eyebrows in expectation.

"I think that's a good idea. Finish eating, then we'll go back to the main house."

Kent smiled. "House is unlocked. Go get whatever you need. And thanks."

"Anytime." I rubbed his shoulder, then looked back at Mason. "You can't swim too long because Poppy is flying in, and we need to pick her up from the airport."

With a taco clutched in one hand, he threw his fists in the sir. "Yes! Today is a really good day. Right, Dad?"

Kent's response was much more subdued. "Sure is."

After cleaning up trash and making sure everyone had gotten food, I drove back to the main house with Mason but made a stop by his house on the way.

While he splashed in the pool, I scratched out the dinner plan for next week. Spending time with Poppy would be different with Mason around, but I didn't have to worry about the conversation lagging. Mason could talk up a storm.

POPPY CURLED up in the overstuffed chair and smiled at Mason who was zonked on the couch. "He's busy and totally adorable. What's their story?"

I didn't want to say more than what Kent was comfortable with people knowing, so I answered carefully. "Mason's mom died last year, and he came to live with Kent. It's been nice having him here on the ranch."

She smiled. "I hope you don't mind that I came to visit again so soon after the wedding."

"Not at all. You're welcome anytime." I checked my phone, hoping I'd hear from Mad Dog or any of the other guys soon.

Sipping her cup of hot tea, she pursed her lips like she was deep in thought. "It's good to see Dad so happy. I grew up hearing stories about his time on the ranch. He loves it here."

"I'm glad. He fit in from day one. He's part of the family now. And so are you. I hope you know that."

Nodding, she smiled. "I love that about this place."

"Tell me about what you do in New York."

Poppy told me all about her big-city job. "I'm not sure how long I'll stay there, but right now I'm happy."

"That's important." I pointed toward the kitchen. "Can I get you anything?"

"No, I'm good." She cradled her mug, looking at me over the rim. "I never thought Dad would marry again. When he called me to tell me he was going to propose, I was so excited. I knew you had to be someone amazing."

"I'm not sure about the amazing part." I risked a question, hoping she wouldn't read my surprise. "He called you before he proposed?"

"He did. I could hear how nervous and excited he was. I think after being married to Mom for almost twenty years, he was afraid to start over. Dating isn't easy at any age, I guess."

"That's true." As if I was any kind of an expert on dating.

"Were you married before?"

"No. I've spent most of my time taking care of cowboys

and ranch hands. That didn't leave me much time for anything else."

"How did you meet Dad?"

"At church. His kindness is rather magnetic. And any time there was a social, he'd eat a slice of pie, and we'd talk."

She blinked. "He ate pie?"

The question was odd, and I hesitated a second before answering. "Yes. Sometimes two slices."

A wide smile spread across her face. "I promise not to barge in too often. But I'm kind of falling in love with this ranch. Tomorrow I'm getting a horseback riding lesson."

"Fun! Parker is a sweetheart. He'll teach you everything you need to know."

"I'm not looking for a sweetheart." She set her cup down and yawned. "I hate to go to bed without telling Dad hello, but I'm about to fall over."

On cue, my phone beeped. "He just texted. Clint is driving him home now."

"Oh, good." She rubbed her face. "Do you need me to help you get Mason home?"

"Kent will probably be here—"

Footsteps sounded on the porch.

"I bet that's him."

I opened the door, and Kent pulled the Stetson off his head as he stepped inside. "I'm sorry to leave him with you all day. Did he behave?"

"He's always a doll. Kent, you remember Poppy, right?" I rubbed his arm. "You okay?"

"Just dead tired." He nodded toward Poppy. "Nice to see you again." When his gaze landed on Mason, Kent smiled. "The way he's growing, I won't be able to carry him much longer."

I didn't miss Poppy doing a quick survey of Kent's arm

muscles. Those biceps could handle a kid five times Mason's size.

"Like a weed." I picked up the little care package I'd put together for them. "In here is dinner for you and breakfast for tomorrow if you decide not to go to the mess hall."

"Thanks, Ava. You're amazing." He scooped Mason off the sofa, then stuck out his hand.

"You carry him. I'll take this." I followed him to the door. "Poppy, I'll be right back." The walk to his place took less than a minute. When we stepped onto the porch, I pushed open the door. "I'll just put this in the kitchen."

"Thanks. Don't leave. I want to ask you something, but let me put him in bed first. I'll be up half the night if he wakes up now."

I set the bag in the kitchen and waited. Outside, a door slammed. Mad Dog was probably home.

Kent walked into the kitchen, dragging his fingers through his hair. "If ever it's inconvenient for you to watch him, please tell me."

"I will. But so far, it's been good."

He emptied the bag of its goodies. "How long is Poppy going to be in town? Mason loves it when she's here."

"She flies out on Monday. Just a short visit." I guessed that Mason wasn't the only one who liked having her around.

"Well, I should let you go, so you can visit." He leaned on the counter. "Just wanted you to know how much I appreciate all you do."

Being a single dad wasn't easy, but Kent never once complained. I was always glad when I could help a little.

I hugged him. "Get some rest."

He walked me to my porch. "Night, Ava."

When I pushed open the front door, I stopped. Mad Dog was standing in the hall with his back to me. Even from behind, I could see how tired he was.

After closing the door quietly, I walked up to him. "Hey there, cowboy." I rubbed his back.

He leaned back into my hand. "That feels good. Poppy just went to bed."

"She was exhausted but waited up to see you. Go shower. I'll make you a quick something." I continued kneading his tired muscles.

"It's like you can read my mind." He turned and wrapped his arms around me. "Today was exhausting, but I'd forgotten how much I love doing that kind of stuff."

"Well, you smell like you've been chasing cattle."

He backed up. "Sorry."

I pulled him close again. "Totally worth the hug. I'll bring food into the bedroom."

Blinking, he bit his lip. But then he turned and walked down the hall. "Thanks."

What didn't he say?

After making him food, I changed into my flannel pajamas. They were a horrible choice for summertime. I'd die of heat exhaustion before the sun came up. But I had to risk it. My big cotton sleepshirt came almost to my knees. It covered way more than anything in Delaney's lingerie shop, but I'd feel almost as exposed as if I were wearing what Joji and Lilith had given me for the wedding. The cotton was so worn, it was almost see-through.

Maybe I'd sweat a few pounds off during the night wearing my flannel pajamas.

The shower shut off, and it was too late to change my mind.

Mad Dog poked his head out. "Did you happen to . . ." He pointed toward the guest room.

"Yes. Sorry." I picked up a pair of boxer briefs off the dresser. "I grabbed some clothes earlier. Here you go." I handed over what I knew he wore to bed.

"I can wear more if you'd like." His voice was soft.

I shook my head. "I wouldn't like."

His chuckle rang out as he closed the door.

Tucked under the covers, I handed him the plate as he climbed into bed. "I know they appreciated your help today."

He nodded as he ate. "It was a good day. Thanks for the food. I was starved. I feel bad for all the other guys."

"I left food in the mess hall fridge. The guys know I'd never let them go hungry." I crossed my arms.

He glanced at me. "I don't mind sleeping on the floor or couch if you are more comfortable with that."

"No. We can share the bed. It's big enough."

Surely, he could read between the lines and understand that I intended to keep my pajamas on. All night.

"Plenty big." He set his empty plate aside, then lay back on the bed and held out his arm. "Come here."

I snuggled up beside him. He could probably feel my heart beating against his side. It took a second before I relaxed enough to rest my head on his chest.

Mad Dog was snoring seconds later.

This was married life. And I loved it.

Whispering into the darkness, I quietly admitted what scared me the most. "I love you."

If he changed his mind now, it would hurt. Deeply and forever. And I still worried he'd wake up one day and decide he didn't want to be married to me anymore.

CHAPTER 26

MAD DOG

The bed shook, and I opened one eye just enough to make out Ava's outline. The faint light of the moon didn't give off enough light to see her in detail. I could only make out her shadow.

She closed herself in the closet, then light could be seen under the door. What was she doing in the closet in the middle of the night?

I pulled the covers up over my shoulder. She kept the air low, and if it weren't for the thick quilt, I'd be freezing.

The light went off, and her shadow emerged from the closet. But her outline was different.

She crawled back into bed.

"Everything okay?" I glanced back over my shoulder.

After a soft gasp, she nodded. "The flannel pajamas were making me hot. I changed into my night shirt. I didn't mean to wake you."

"It's fine."

For several minutes, we both lay there silently. She was awake. I could tell from the way she was breathing.

The covers shifted, and I worried for a second she was going to get out of bed and find somewhere else to sleep.

"It's been a long time since I've shared a bed." My whispered statement shattered the stillness.

"Years ago, before my father walked out, my mom would sleep in my bed on nights he was out getting drunk. That's the only time I've ever had anyone else in my bed." The covers moved. "It's just different."

"Good different, I hope."

"Yes." She shifted close to my back and pressed her cheek to my skin. "Good night."

I lay awake until her breathing changed and she was sound asleep. "Love you, Ava."

THE SUN WASN'T YET up when I opened my eyes. Living with Ava had changed my internal clock. I rarely slept past sunrise.

Her breath tickled my back, and I stayed as still as possible. I hoped we'd soon be at a place where this was part of every morning. It had been a long time since I'd shared a bed, and I missed it. There was a quiet magic in listening to her relaxed breathing.

When she shifted, I rolled to my back, hoping she'd snuggle up to me.

Instead, concern etched on her face. "I'm sorry for crowding you." She moved toward the opposite edge of the bed.

"You aren't crowding me. Don't get up. Can we talk for a minute? I fell asleep on you last night. I'm sorry."

She eased closer to me. "Technically, I fell asleep on you. Literally and when we were awake in the middle of the night."

"It was nice." I stretched out my arm. "How did yesterday go with Poppy? I didn't mean to be absent all day."

She snuggled in like she had last night. "Mason was around most of the day, but we talked for a little while after he went to sleep. She's fantastic with Mason. Maybe she'll give you grandkids one day. She'll be a great mom."

I ran my fingers through Ava's hair, enjoying the rare treat of seeing it down. "Maybe she'll give *us* grandkids."

She sniffed. "Right. I hadn't thought of that. And months ago I thought Mason was as close as I'd come to having grandkids."

"You don't look old enough to be a grandma."

Ava stayed quiet for a minute before speaking again. "She also said that you called her and told her you were going to propose. I wasn't sure when you had time for that. I guess I thought you'd made your final decision after waking up that morning." She avoided my gaze as she asked the question.

I kissed her forehead. "I waited because I wanted you to have time to change your mind."

"I'm glad I didn't."

"Me too. I have a question for you. And I want your honest opinion." I'd been noodling an idea, but if she didn't like the plan, I needed to stop thinking about it.

"Okay?"

"Jeffrey and I had lunch one day this week, and he was talking about how the foreman he's had for many years is planning to quit. Jeffrey stays busy with the restaurant, but he doesn't want to get rid of the family ranch. He needs someone to run things. It's not nearly as big as what Beau has. Anyway, what would you think of me giving up my job at the church and going to work for him? I haven't even mentioned it to him. I'd probably make a little bit less than what I make at the church, but I have money put away. I wouldn't be a financial drain on you."

She sucked in a breath and stayed very still. "You'd stop being a pastor?"

I wanted to retract my words, but it was too late. "Not completely. I'd still do weddings and fill in when Gary needed me."

She pushed off my chest and sat up. "Are you doing this because he wants to come out of retirement?"

"If you don't like the idea, I'll drop it."

She shook her head. "I didn't say I didn't like it. It's just . . ." Her brow furrowed, and she pinched her lips together before snuggling back against me. "I thought you really wanted to keep your job at the church."

What an idiot I was!

She'd married me so that I wouldn't lose my job, and here I was talking about giving it up.

"It's not that I don't like what I do. I'll just keep being a pastor. We don't have to make any big changes." I went back to stroking her hair. "I just wanted your opinion."

To me, sharing a bed felt like a big change, but that was only temporary and way off topic.

"Talk to the higher ups and to Jeffrey. I'll be happy no matter what you choose to do."

"By higher ups, do you mean at the church or"—I pointed upwards—"the Big Guy upstairs?"

She rolled her eyes.

I pulled her a little closer. "You'll stay married to me if I choose to be a full-time cowboy?"

She nodded, and her long hair tickled my chest. "I should get up. We need to eat before church."

"Is Poppy going with us?" I didn't expect her to, but making assumptions had gotten me in trouble more than once.

Ava grinned. "She's getting a riding lesson from Parker. But guess who else is getting a riding lesson this morning?"

"Is he short and has a dad who avoids looking my daughter in the eye?"

"Yep. I'm guessing that poor Kent is planning to go along and has no idea about Poppy." Ava patted my chest. "I'm getting up. Want me to bring you coffee in bed?"

"Wow. Today is turning out to be awesome."

She climbed out of bed and looked back over her shoulder. "I'm guessing that's a yes."

"You're beautiful."

A blush made her even more attractive. "Flattery will get you coffee *and* breakfast in bed." She blew me a kiss as she walked out of the room.

Soon, I needed to tell Ava I was in love. Picking the perfect time was key. I didn't want her to think I was saying it so that I could get something else in bed.

Not that I didn't want that. But intimacy had to be her choice. And if telling her I loved her made her feel pressured, I'd keep my mouth shut a little longer.

But it was getting harder. More than once, I'd almost slipped and told her.

AFTER THINKING about the job situation for two days, I made a decision. Waiting in the dark for my friend to finish up at work made me look like a stalker, but I'd told him I'd meet him, so that nullified the stalker bit.

I jumped out of the truck as Jeffrey walked out of the restaurant. It was late, but I wanted to catch him before he hired someone else.

"Hey." He raked his fingers through his hair. "How are you? Poppy make it home okay?"

"She did. Good flight. I'm guessing she'll be back soon." I dropped the tailgate and sat down.

He sat at the other end. "And are you back in the guest room?"

"I don't want to talk about that. I wanted to talk about—"

He laughed. "You could've just said yes. You know, I've been thinking about our conversation the other day. About how you are bad at flirting."

"Jeffrey, that's not important right now."

"I think it is. You are horrible at dating. You lack self-confidence. You can't flirt worth a darn. But I think you are good at being married. So maybe—just maybe—this whole backward thing will work in your favor." He crossed his arms, punctuating his point.

"That might be the wisest thing you've ever said."

He grinned. "Told you it was important. What did you want to tell me?"

"Have you hired someone for the foreman job?"

Pointing at the restaurant, he shook his head. "That eats up all my time, remember? But it's on my list. Why?"

I swallowed. "I want the job."

He scrubbed his face and didn't answer for several seconds. "Have you talked to Ava about this? You don't even know what it pays."

"I'd need to know those kinds of details. And, yes, I talked to Ava."

"The Ava who married you so that you wouldn't lose your job as the pastor."

"Yes, Jeffrey. That Ava. I didn't plan it this way, but maybe she'll realize that I wanted her more than the job."

"You could just tell her that. You know, with words."

"Thanks for the advice." I sighed. "Text me and let me know when you want to talk about the job."

Jeffrey patted my shoulder. "I will. Go home to your wife." Chuckling, he slid off the tailgate. "If you're worried that she doesn't feel the way you do, don't. I have a sense for these things. She loves you. It's obvious."

"A sense, huh?"

"Yep. I can always tell when a woman isn't interested. She rolls her eyes in that bothered sort of way and sighs like I'm using up good air. Ava doesn't do that when you're around. That's got to be good."

"I hope you're right." I shook his hand, then climbed into my truck.

Deep inside, I knew he was right. Ava loved me. But she wasn't quite ready to let herself be fully loved.

For some it was easier to give than to receive.

CHAPTER 27

AVA

*T*hursday afternoon, I poked my head into Beau's office. "Any applicants?"

He shook his head. "If you can think of other places to list the ad, I'm open to that. We've had one call about the job. She said she was too educated to clean toilets."

"Whatever that means."

"It means she isn't getting the job." He came around the desk. "I'm sorry it's taking so long."

"That's okay. It'll all work out." I checked my phone when it beeped. "Mason skinned up his knee. I'm going to go patch it up."

"Don't know what we'd do without you around here." He grinned. "You are equal parts angel and bear."

"Thanks, I guess." Laughing, I hurried out to the mess hall after grabbing the first aid kit.

Mason sat in a chair. His jeans were torn, and tears streaked down his face.

Kent squatted beside him. "Miss Ava is going to fix it up, bud. You'll be okay."

Mason sniffled. "I know."

I pulled a chair in front of him. "Kent, will you grab the jar of magic cookies out of the last cabinet on the right? Mason will need those." I surveyed his wound. "While you munch on those cookies, I'm going to clean the scrape before patching it up."

Kent handed Mason two cookies.

With one in each hand, he put on a brave face. "I'm ready now."

I cleaned off the dirt and blood, and Kent kept handing over cookies.

By the time I had a bandage on Mason's knee, the kid had eaten seven cookies.

"Does that feel better?" I kissed the top of his head.

He nodded. "Thank you, Miss Ava."

Whistling sounded outside, and I smiled. Mad Dog was here.

He walked into the mess hall. "No one invited me to the party."

Mason giggled. "We aren't having a party. Miss Ava was fixin' up my knee."

"What happened?"

He glanced at his dad. "I was chasing one of the barn cats, and I tripped."

"Does the cat like it when you chase him?" Kent's tone was gentle.

"No. He doesn't." Mason's shoulder sagged. "I shouldn't have done it."

Mad Dog rubbed Mason's shoulder. "It's very grown up of you to admit that. Did Ava get you feeling better?"

"Yep. She let me have lots of magic cookies." The kid grinned, then with a straight face turned to his dad. "Can we go back to the barn? I want to say sorry to the cat."

"Sure thing, kiddo." Kent took Mason's hand, and they walked out.

Mad Dog grabbed a cookie out of the jar. "These really are magic cookies, aren't they?"

"That's why I call them that. Have as many as you want." In the closet, I loaded my bucket with cleaning supplies.

Mad Dog stepped up beside me. "Have another bucket?"

"Yes, why?"

"You clean here at the main house. I'll take care of the ranch hands' cabins." He leaned against the door frame. "If my cleaning skills are up to snuff."

"You took the day off."

"Because I had a few things to do, and I got some of them done this morning. I'm not going to work with the guys because I'm meeting the realtor later this afternoon, and I don't want to smell like I've been rubbing up against cows. But I have time to clean before my appointment."

"The realtor?" I filled a second bucket. "Did you decide to sell the house?"

"It's paid off, so it makes more sense to rent it out for now. But I'm going to let her handle all that. She does property management as well as buying and selling."

"Oh, good." I hugged him. "Thank you for offering to clean. It's sweet. You take good care of me."

He kept his arm around me. "I promise to always try."

THAT EVENING MAD Dog wandered into the kitchen. "Would you like a glass of wine?"

"Sure." I'd only have one. More than that would not be wise. I'd probably end up in his lap, asking him to move into my room.

I was not ready for that.

After Poppy left, he went back to sleeping in the guest room without saying anything about it. I wasn't sure if I should be relieved that I didn't have to ask him to go back to the guest room or offended that he didn't even ask to stay in my room.

Worrying about it was silly.

He poured two glasses then pointed toward the couch. "I wanted to tell you how today went."

"Right. What did the realtor say?"

"She thinks it will rent quickly." He clasped my hand. "So I wanted to doublecheck with you before I signed off on that. If I rent the place, I won't have any place to go if . . ." He shrugged. "I think you know what I mean."

How could he think I didn't want him here?

"Currently, I have no plans to toss you out." I grinned so he'd know I was trying to be funny.

"That's what I was hoping you'd say." He kissed my hand. "Poppy called today. Said she enjoyed her visit. She really likes you."

"I like her too. It's a shame she doesn't live closer."

"I know." He finished off his wine. "I think instead of calling the district office to let them know I plan to step down I should talk to them in person. I'm going to call tomorrow and see what days they have open on their schedule, then I'll drive up to Austin."

"I'm excited for you. It's a big change. I'm sure Jeffrey is thrilled."

"He is. Maybe one weekend I can take you over there so that you can see the place."

"I'd love that. Is it close?"

"Very. His ranch is a stone's throw from the entrance to the venue on the other end of the ranch."

"It's worked out so perfectly."

"We just need to find you some help, then it will all be perfect." He covered a yawn.

Life had changed so much in such a short time. I owed it

all to lemon bars. Was it wrong of me not to want to ask Mrs. Beecham for her recipe?

With a little trial and error, I could find a good recipe and tweak it until it was perfect . . . or at least better than hers.

That woman brought out my petty side.

CHAPTER 28

MAD DOG

I called Ava as soon as I was back in my truck. "The meeting went smoothly. They asked that I be available for the next few weeks to help with Gary's transition, but it's all coming together. Officially my last day is the Sunday after next."

"Oh, Mad Dog. That's wonderful. I'm so happy for you."

Without her, none of this would've happened. When I moved out to the ranch and had a taste of ranching again, I wanted a change. But the biggest change was marrying her.

Did I wish that I'd asked her out ages ago like a normal person?

Yes.

Was I sorry about how things had worked out?

Not at all.

Maybe after my job at the church was done and all hints of scandal didn't matter, I could be a little more honest with Ava. The romance between us had continued to grow. And she'd seemed almost disappointed when I went into the guest room Monday night.

I missed having her snuggled up beside me.

"I'll be home in a few hours." After driving up last night, I missed her more than I'd expected.

"I can't wait to see you. The guys are having pizza tonight, so I'll be here when you get home. And I have a surprise."

I liked the sound of that. "Do I get a hint?"

"Nope. Drive safely."

I caught myself before saying 'Love you.' "See you soon."

My phone rang as I turned out of the lot. I answered on Blue Tooth. "Jeffrey, it's official. I hope you aren't calling because you changed your mind."

"Sounds like it's too late for that. But no. I'm really happy about this."

"I appreciate you giving me a chance."

"Yeah, well, I did some asking around before hiring you." His laugh sounded nervous.

It was a short list of possibilities. "Did you talk to Clint or Beau?"

"Clint. Now that he doesn't think I'm trying to date Joji, we are kind of friendly. He's a good guy."

"You wanted to date Joji?"

"A little. She's pretty cute, but I don't think it would've worked out." There was a hint of mischief in his tone.

I wasn't going to miss a great opportunity to tease. "Because she was in love with Clint?"

"Because she has too many opinions."

I laughed. "And you wonder why you've had so much trouble finding a wife."

"Shocker, isn't it? This weekend I want to have you and Ava over. I was thinking Sunday afternoon."

"I'll talk to her and get back to you on that." I was excited to begin this next chapter of my life.

After fighting traffic most of the way home, I was eager for the quiet of the ranch. Living in a small town was great; living on the ranch was even better.

When I got to the house, there was a note on the door. *Had to run to the mess hall. Be home soon.*

I'd make use of the time and take a quick shower.

After a short but much-needed shower, I wrapped a towel around myself. In my haste, I'd forgotten to grab clothes. But if Ava had made it home already, it wouldn't be the first time she'd seen me in a towel.

I stepped into the hall just as Ava walked out of the kitchen.

"I worked all afternoon, but I think I perfected the recipe." She hurried toward me with a tray in one hand and a lemon bar in the other. Only steps away, she toppled forward.

Stopping her fall wasn't possible, but breaking it was. I let go of my towel and held out my arms to catch her on the way down.

We landed in a heap with lemon bars beneath us, between us, and on top of us.

I'd need another shower.

"I'm so sorry." She started to push up, then dropped back against my chest. "You dropped your towel."

"You dropped your lemon bars." I kissed a smudge of lemon off the corner of her mouth.

She froze half a second before she kissed me back. We lay on the floor in the hall, enjoying the taste of lemon on each other's lips.

When a knock sounded, she giggled. "I hope that isn't Mason."

"You and me both." I reached over to grab the towel just in case.

The door swung open. "Ava?" Clint called out.

He wouldn't be here long. Only as long as it took to spot us on the floor.

And as soon as his gaze landed on us, the door slammed.

From behind it, he yelled, "Start locking your door!"

"Or maybe wait until someone answers before coming in." Ava giggled again. "I think he just learned that lesson."

"I learned something too." I swiped another bit of the lemon filling off her cheek.

"That lemon bars are bad luck?"

"I think you meant to say good luck. And I think these bars taste better than the ones Mrs. Beecham made."

Ava kissed me again, and we spent another few minutes on the floor.

"I'll cover my eyes. You go get back into the shower." Her hands covered most of her face, and if she was peeking, I couldn't tell. I hoped she was. That would be even more progress.

Sadly, that night, she crawled into her bed alone and didn't invite me to join her.

~

Sunday afternoon Ava walked out of the bedroom wearing a summery cotton dress. "I'm ready."

"Do you have your swimsuit on under that?" I buttoned up my Hawaiian shirt.

"I'm not parading around his house in a swimsuit. Y'all can swim." She crossed her arms.

I knew better than to argue. "All right."

It bothered me that she didn't want to be seen in a swimsuit. I loved the way she looked, and Jeffrey didn't care. But saying that wouldn't help. I'd been married long enough to know that.

She was quiet on the drive to Jeffrey's, and I was glad it wasn't far away.

Since the second lemon bar incident, there were times when Ava had been strangely quiet. It was a different quiet from before, and she'd glance at me during those times. And sometimes her gaze would linger. I wished her thoughts appeared in a bubble above her head.

Curiosity was eating at me.

When I pulled up to Jeffrey's place, an unfamiliar car was parked in front. Who else had he invited?

I helped Ava out of the truck. "I think someone else might be here, but I'm not sure who."

Giggling sounded from near the pool as we walked around the house.

Ava rolled her eyes. "Sounds like Jeffrey met someone. Young." The last word was clearly a jab.

I shot her a surprised look.

She slapped a hand over her mouth. "I'm sorry. That was really rude. I haven't even met her."

"I'm not judging. It just surprised me to hear you saying it."

A woman in a string bikini stood in front of Jeffrey, gazing up at him as if he hung the moon. She was young. And she was giggling.

"Mad Dog, you made it!" Jeffrey sighed as soon as she was behind him. "Ava, hi. This is my friend Layla. We met this morning when I was buying steaks."

Jeffrey was a nice guy, but he made horrible decisions when it came to women.

"Nice to meet you, Layla." Ava stuck out her hand. There was no edge to her voice.

"You too. I just moved here. Since I hardly know anyone, Jeffrey invited me over. Did you know that he's a chef? I read about him on the internet."

Later I'd have fun teasing my friend.

"He's a great chef." Ava set her purse in a chair. "Where did you move from?"

While Ava talked with Layla, I followed Jeffrey inside to get the food. "You met her this morning?"

"It was early. She's short and cute. I hadn't had coffee. And I woke up lonely. So shoot me." He piled the steaks on a tray. "She doesn't have many opinions though."

"Everything you do is great?"

"Something like that." He scanned the tray and mumbled to himself.

"Boring, isn't it?"

"Totally. Open the door for me, will you?"

When we walked back out, Ava was seated on the edge of the pool, dangling her feet in the water. Layla was bobbing up and down, talking.

Jeffrey stopped beside the grill. "Is she always that nice?"

"You mean Ava?"

"Who else would I be talking about? You only just met Layla."

"Hold the snark." I glanced back at Ava, and she smiled. "And, yes, she's that nice most of the time. Helping people comes naturally to her."

"Does she have any friends? I'm open to women with opinions." He smirked. "But only a few."

"I'll let you know."

CHAPTER 29

AVA

*W*ith pies set out on the cooling racks, I set a sign in front of each one. *DO NOT TOUCH.*

There was no way I was buying pies for Mad Dog's party. Gary was excited about working again, and Mad Dog was like a kid waiting for Christmas.

Ever since dropping the lemon bars in the hall, I'd given a lot of thought to inviting him back into my bedroom. Even as dense as I could be, I knew it was cruel to ask the man to sleep beside me and only cuddle. But I'd decided I wanted more than that.

"Did you make enough pies? You must've started baking before the sun came up." Lilith strolled up to the counter.

"I've been up since four. The reception is at ten this morning. And I wanted the pies to be fresh."

"I like the signs." She laughed.

"I learned my lesson. I haven't made pies since that day. It's been too long."

She nodded. "Beau thought you were trying to punish him by depriving him of pie."

"No. I just . . ." My reasoning made no sense. "I don't

know. Pies made me think of what happened. And I didn't want to think about that."

She lifted on eyebrow. "So what changed?"

"Me." I'd made an array of pies, planning to admit to Mad Dog what I wanted and how I felt.

I wanted to be his wife in every sense of the word.

Lilith didn't need to know that part.

"Think it's the well water here on the ranch, or what?" She picked up an apple out of the basket.

I could pretend I had no idea what she meant, but in a weird way, she made perfect sense. "Maybe it is the water. If Beau ever wanted to rent out those cabins, he could put a tagline in the ad: *Our special water makes love grow.*"

"That would bring in hordes of people. For me, it's the moon and stars. Staring up at them quiets my mind and makes it easier to know what's important."

"I like that way of looking at it."

Years ago, when the house was full of people, I'd go out to the little cabin to quiet my mind. When I lived alone, my house was my retreat. But over the last couple of months, the time spent with Mad Dog was when my mind quieted and my soul found its calm.

"Don't wait until you think you're going to lose him to say what you need to say." Lilith smiled before biting into her apple.

The oven timer went off, and I was saved from having to respond. She was right. And after the party, Mad Dog and I needed to have a long-overdue conversation.

I EXPECTED that everyone and their dog (pun intended) would turn out to wish Mad Dog well on his next adventure.

I wasn't sure who knew what that next adventure was because he'd been quiet about his plans.

Mrs. Beecham would probably be horrified, and that thought made me giggle.

The fellowship hall was all set up. I scanned the tables, making sure nothing had been missed. Pie servers! Without those, people would be struggling to get pie. Or the kids would scoop it out with their hands. In the kitchen closet, I dug through the bin of serving utensils, trying to find every last pie server.

After finding several, I grabbed a stack of napkins. People would be a mess without these. A voice stopped me before I stepped back into the kitchen.

"I'm guessing his leaving is all Ava's doing." Mrs. Beecham sounded meaner than normal. "He only married her because he caught us saying that no one would marry Ava. Maybe he thinks that makes him a good person. Or maybe he did it out of spite."

I grabbed the wall and held my breath. I didn't want to get caught listening.

"He probably thinks he's a modern-day Hosea." She huffed.

Tears burned my eyes, but I couldn't cry now. Not here.

"I think you're wrong." Goldie's tone was soft but firm. "You choose to see the worst in people, but you're wrong about Mad Dog and about Ava."

Footsteps sounded, but I wasn't sure if they'd both left. The last thing I wanted was to come face to face with Mrs. Beecham right now.

How long could I hide in the closet?

A door closed, and I peeked out. I'd never been so happy to see an empty kitchen. After counting to ten, I carried the pie servers and napkins out to the table.

"Oh. There you are. My lemon bars should go here in the center of the table. I moved the pies over there."

Mrs. Beecham had to be unhappy. Almost everything out of her mouth was bitter and hurtful.

I didn't have to respond in the same way. "Good idea. They are delicious. Best I've ever tasted." That was only a tiny fib. Mine were better, but I wasn't going to tell her that.

She rolled her eyes. "Please tell me you didn't eat them off the floor."

Telling her that I kissed them off the side of Mad Dog's face was tempting. But I didn't. It wasn't true, and I didn't want her to go into cardiac arrest at church. I'd feel guilty about that.

Smiling, I laid the napkins on the table. "If you see anything else I missed, let me know."

Goldie waved from the other side of the room, and I made my escape.

"Hi!" She cut a glance at Mrs. Beecham, then stepped closer. "How are you? The news about Mad Dog leaving is quite a shock."

"He'll still be around. He just won't be preaching."

Her eyebrows lifted. "Can I ask what he'll be doing?"

"Ranching." I put a finger to my lips. "But he's keeping that quiet for now."

"Are you going to continue working? I saw the ad about needing help at the ranch. In fact, I was going to apply if you haven't found someone already."

"I'm not going anywhere, but the job is too big for one person. And we haven't filled the slot. We need a housekeeper and also someone who will cook on the weekends." I clasped her hand. "Call me and we'll set up an interview."

"I'd appreciate that. My company had layoffs, and I was one of the lucky ones." She smiled, but the worry in her eyes was unmistakable. "I'll call you."

I needed to talk to Beau before offering, but letting Goldie live in one of the cabins would make it easier for her to handle breakfast on the weekends. And it would help her budget.

Crowds packed into the room, and the pies started to disappear. I needed to get Mad Dog a slice before there wasn't anything left. Thinking back to all the times he'd eaten pie, I tried to remember what kind he ate most often. He never ate the crust on the apple pie, so I skipped over that one. Pecan pie. Who didn't like pecan pie? He'd eaten that one before.

I cut a large slice, then set off to find him.

He was talking with a woman from the church. She was young and gorgeous, but I tried not to focus on that.

Smiling, he extended his hand as I walked up. "Hi, sweetheart."

"I didn't mean to interrupt, but I wanted to give you a slice of pie before it all got eaten." I held out the plate.

"No thanks." He shook his head, then motioned to the woman. "Would you like pie?"

"Yes." She took the plate. "Pecan is my favorite."

"Great." What else was I supposed to say?

But everything wasn't great. Mad Dog had never before turned down a slice of my pie. My mind jumped to what I'd overheard in the kitchen, and the pieces fit in a heart-breaking way.

As I stepped away, he caught my arm. "Is everything okay?"

"Yes. I need to go check the kitchen." Lying was the only way to get out of here without embarrassing myself, and I'd done enough of that.

Hearing that he'd only married me because of sour gossips felt true now.

And now that he wasn't the pastor, it didn't matter what

people thought. There was no need for him to be married to avoid a scandal. But because he was so kind, he'd go right on pretending. Doing exactly what he'd told me not to do in the very beginning.

Feeling like a whale of a charity case, I slipped out the back door. It was good that we'd come in separate trucks. Logistics was the reason, but now, I could escape without having to call Joji or Lilith.

They'd only try to talk me out of leaving.

I needed to think.

At the house, I changed into jeans. Crossing the river in a dress begged for disaster. Unsuccessfully trying to hold back tears, I stopped at the mess hall and grabbed a box of cookies, two bags of chips, a bag of chocolates, a Dr Pepper, and an apple. The kind of thinking I needed to do required sustenance.

"I thought you'd be at church." Beau sometimes showed up at the worst times.

"I was." Smiling, I wiped my face. "I'll see you later."

"Ava, wait." His brow pinched. "What's wrong?"

"Nothing." I hurried out before he could ask any more questions.

I pulled away from the house.

There were no vehicles parked near the storage shed, which was good. I dug out the canoe and dragged it to the truck. Before leaving, I grabbed a length of rope just in case.

Crossing the river was a must, and I wasn't sure how hard it would be. But I needed my quiet place to figure out how to tell Mad Dog that he was free. I didn't want to be the woman he married out of kindness. I wasn't going to keep him trapped.

Refusing the pie felt personal.

Instead of telling him I loved him, I'd tell him I didn't

want to be married to him anymore. But it would take a lot of thought and mustered courage to get those words out.

I backed up to the river's edge, tossed my snacks and the rope into the canoe, and got ready to cross the river. In my haste, I'd made a grievous error. I hadn't grabbed oars. The boat was useless if I didn't have a way of propelling it across the water.

Scanning the river, I concocted a plan. Once upon a time, I'd been great at lassoing. But that was years ago.

"Please let me have enough skill left to snag that stump." I tied the rope, then flung it.

It didn't even make it halfway across the river.

This was the narrowest spot. I either made it work here, or I had to go back for the oars. By now, Mad Dog might have noticed that I'd left.

And I did not want to be found.

I pitched the rope again and landed it perfectly on the stump. Carefully, I climbed into the canoe and pulled myself across the river. As soon as I touched the dirt, I jumped out and dragged the canoe into the grass.

With my arms full of snacks, I trekked through the trees to my cabin. It was worse than I'd expected. The roof had caved in on one side, and some of the walls looked like a strong wind would blow them over.

After testing the front step to be sure it wouldn't collapse, I sat down on the porch. At least that hadn't fallen apart.

CHAPTER 30

MAD DOG

$\mathcal{A}$fter a half hour of chatting and shaking hands, I went in search of something to drink, hoping I'd find Ava as well. I hadn't seen her since she'd offered me pie. She wasn't manning the serving tables, and she wasn't in the kitchen.

I gave up my search for a drink. A knot formed in the pit of my stomach. Something had been wrong when she walked away earlier. I should've listened to my gut.

After checking my office and the janitor's closet, I ran out to the parking lot. If her truck wasn't here, I wouldn't waste my time searching the rest of the building.

Her truck was gone. Without bothering to run back inside and say any proper goodbyes, I jumped into my truck and drove back to the ranch.

What had her so upset that she'd leave without telling me?

Did Mrs. Beecham say something ugly or mean?

By the time I pulled onto the ranch, the knot in my stomach had doubled in size. And when I saw that her truck wasn't parked in front of our house, the knot twisted as it grew. Where was she?

I knocked on Kent's door, and when he answered, I didn't wait for him to say anything. "Have you seen Ava?"

"I haven't seen her since this morning. Parker is on his way over. I can ask him."

"Thanks! I'm going to go check at the main house." I ran back to my truck, wondering if I'd done something wrong.

Her truck wasn't at the main house, but maybe someone knew where she was. I prayed that I'd bump into Beau and not Clint.

Today wasn't my lucky day.

"Hey, I thought you had that thing at church." Clint waved as he walked toward me.

"I did. Have you seen Ava?"

His eyes narrowed. "What happened?"

"I don't know." I didn't care if I sounded desperate. "She left the church without saying anything to me, and she isn't at home."

Beau sauntered around the corner of the house. "Why do y'all look so serious? And aren't you supposed to be at church?"

"Yes. I'm supposed to be at church." I raked my fingers through my hair. "I'm trying to find Ava. Have you seen her?"

He nodded. "A bit ago. She was in the mess hall." His lips pulled into a straight line. "She was crying and gathering snacks. What did you do?" His accusation was blatant and probably deserved.

"I don't know!" Rubbing my temples, I looked out toward the barn. "Where could she be? Will you check with Lilith and Joji?"

The guys whipped out their phones.

Clint shook his head. "She isn't with Joji."

"Lilith is at the venue. Says she hasn't seen Ava since this morning." Beau flashed an apologetic smile. "I'm not sure where she'd be. Usually if she isn't cleaning or cooking, she's at home."

"And I was just up at the ranch hands' cabins. She wasn't there." Clint shoved his hands into his pockets. "What was the last thing that happened?"

"I told her I didn't want any pie."

Beau scratched his head. "That doesn't even make sense. How could you not want any pie?"

"Can we please stop talking about pie? I want to find Ava. I need to think." The words echoed in my head, and I grabbed Clint's arm. "There's a cabin where she used to go. By the river."

"It's probably dilapidated. Why would she go there?"

"She liked to go there to think." I yanked my keys back out of my pocket. "How do I get there?"

"You don't. The bridge washed out years ago. There isn't even a good trail to that place from the main road." Beau wasn't being helpful.

"Just point me toward the river. I'll figure something out. I'm almost sure she's over there." I'd beg if I had to.

Clint walked toward his truck. "Beau, you ride with Mad Dog. I'll meet y'all at the narrow spot." He turned and pointed at us. "Stop and get the canoe on your way."

Beau jumped into the passenger seat as I slid in behind the wheel.

"Tell me where to go." If I didn't find her soon, I was going to lose my mind, and that wouldn't be pretty.

Following Beau's directions, I made it to a shed.

"Wait here a sec." He hopped out but returned a minute later. "Canoe is gone. You might be right about where she is."

We continued to the river, and as soon as we arrived, Clint pulled up and parked next to us.

"That's her truck. She's around here somewhere." He looked into the bed of the truck. "Where's the boat?"

"There." I pointed to the other side of the river.

The canoe was pulled up on shore. One end of a rope was tied to the boat. The other end was lassoed around a stump.

"Dang. She's still got it." Clint chuckled. "I'd forgotten how good she was with a lasso."

"Good to know." I was beginning to wonder what else there was about Ava that I didn't know.

After pacing along the bank, I kicked off my shoes. "Okay, when I get to the other side, which way is it to the cabin?"

"You don't want to swim here. Especially not in that suit." Beau shaded his eyes and looked across to the other side. "She really wants to be alone, I guess."

"Not an option. Unless you guys have a better idea, I'm going to jump in." I emptied my pockets.

"Put your shoes back on. You'll want them on when you're walking to the cabin." Clint walked to the bed of his truck. "I grabbed the extension ladder just in case. It's not really designed to be used like a bridge, but in a pinch it'll have to do. Either that, or we drive around, but that'll take another ten minutes." He extended the ladder out as far as it would go, then he and Beau laid it out over the water. It was just long enough so that it rested on the bank on the opposite side.

"The sooner I get over there, the better."

"I suggest you don't dilly-dally near the middle. I'm not sure it'll hold you for long in that spot." Clint clapped me on the back. "When you get to the other side, cut to the right and go about two hundred feet. The cabin will be on your left, nestled in a stand of trees. Good luck."

"Thanks." With all my worrying, I hadn't even thought about what to say to her.

"I hope you find her soon because we planned a surprise

thing for you." Beau rubbed his face. "So when you get this all cleared up, you can meet us at the pool."

"Okay." I scrambled across the ladder, holding my breath as I crossed the middle. The creaking worried me, but I kept moving. Stopping now would only land me in the water.

I wanted to be with Ava. Whatever had upset her needed to be fixed. I just needed to figure out how.

I breathed a sigh of relief when I stepped onto the opposite shore, and my shoes squished into the muddy bank.

Beau waved. "That's our lucky ladder!"

"Did you notice that he waited until you made it across to tell you that?" Clint laughed. "Go find her."

I flashed them a thumbs up before darting off through the trees. After a short distance, I walked into an open pasture. Butterflies hovered over a field of wildflowers. The air was alive with the sounds of insects and birds.

Too distracted to know how far I'd run, I kept scanning the area, hoping to spot a clue. A loud pop sounded.

Birds fluttered out of the trees. And I froze.

It didn't quite sound like a gunshot, but what was it? Whatever it was, it was close.

After a deep breath, hoping to slow down my heart rate, I glanced around. A bag of chips lay on the ground. I'd stepped on it and popped it open.

Ava must've dropped some of her snacks. She had to be close.

I cut to the left, and after only a few paces, I saw the cabin peeking through the trees.

It had seen better days. I was surprised to see Ava sitting on the porch. She was braver than I was.

A half-full Dr Pepper and a bag of chips lay next to her. With a bag of chocolates in one hand, she was staring off into the trees and popping chocolates into her mouth with the other hand.

My heart broke to see her so upset. "I'd sit next to you, but I'm afraid the house would topple over."

Her head snapped around. "How'd you get here?"

"I used the lucky ladder." Based on the way the guys talked about it, there had to be a funny story, right?

Instead of laughing, like I hoped, Ava launched off the porch and marched into the trees. "I hate that ladder."

I'd never seen Ava so hard and cold, but the tear stains on her cheeks told a different part of the story.

Leaves crunched beneath my feet as I walked toward her. "Will you tell me why you're upset?"

She crossed her arms and leaned back against a tree. "I hope you didn't tell Beau where I keep that ladder. Every time it gets pulled out, someone gets hurt."

"Clint grabbed the ladder. He didn't say where he'd gotten it." Positioning myself right in front of her, I leaned down until I was eye-level with her. "Did I do something to hurt you?"

Her chin quivered, and she looked over my shoulder toward the cabin. "When I used to come out here years ago, I scrubbed the entire cabin and hung little curtains in the windows. There was no furniture inside, so Clint made me a small bench." She wiped at a tear. "I regret not getting it out before the place fell apart. But even when I was spending so much time cleaning it up, I knew that someday the cabin would end up dilapidated. There was no way to stop the weather from beating on it. The cabin would one day fall over or be torn down. It was inevitable."

I listened, trying to understand how what she said about the cabin applied to why she was upset.

Her gaze snapped to mine. "So I don't blame you. It was inevitable."

"What?"

She turned and picked bark off the tree. "I overheard

ladies talking at church . . . in the kitchen." After a brief glance over her shoulder, she continued. "I went into the closet to get pie servers and napkins. They didn't know I was in there."

Anger bubbled in my gut. What horrible thing had those women said?

She blew out a breath, then marched back to the porch and picked up a handful of chocolates. "Mrs. Beecham said you heard ladies saying that no one would marry me."

"You shouldn't—" I stopped, wishing I knew what magic words to say to her.

"Did you?" Ava blinked and popped a chocolate into her mouth.

I hated that she was insulating because of me. She was insulating herself from me.

Telling the truth would only complicate the situation, but I wouldn't lie to Ava. "Yes, but that wasn't why I asked you to marry me."

She unwrapped another chocolate. "Well, now that you aren't the pastor, it won't matter if we stay married. I can ask Beau about letting you live in one of the cabins."

I wasn't giving up that easily. I'd eat pie for another ten years if need be. "Are you dying?"

Her brows pinched. "No."

"Neither am I. And I meant 'till death do us part.' So why are we talking about not being married?"

She dropped back onto the step and buried her face in her hands. Sobs broke loose, and she struggled to catch her breath. I was glad her brother was far away on the other side of the river because this scene would get me into trouble.

I waited to hear what horrible thing I'd said or done. Seeing her upset made me ill. Knowing I was the reason made retching much more likely. But I didn't know why. And that frustrated me.

Ignoring the risk, I sat down beside her on the front step and reached for her hand. "Please talk to me."

She stared at her fingers in my hand but didn't pull away. "You don't even want my pies anymore."

I laughed, which was the worst possible choice for that moment.

An eerie creak sounded when she shoved off the step and headed back toward the trees.

I chased after her, glad to be off the porch but sorry I'd upset her. This time, the truth might prove beneficial. "Ava, will you look at me?"

Tears brimmed in her brown eyes.

I touched her arm. "I don't like pie."

"What? But you used to . . ." She unwrapped another chocolate and stared at the cabin.

"I used to eat pie so I could talk to you. For months I wanted to ask you out, but I'm not great when it comes to dating. And I chickened out." I stepped closer. "Please don't go back and sit on that porch. Getting emergency vehicles over here would be difficult at best."

She handed me the chocolate. "You ate pie you didn't like so that you could talk to me?"

Why had I waited so long to say this to her? "Yes. And I'm fully aware of how pitiful that makes me sound."

"You were afraid to ask me out?" She chewed her bottom lip.

"I'd like to have a grand story about why I delayed asking you out on a date, but you pretty much summed it up correctly. I was afraid of being rejected."

"But you asked me to marry you."

"You brought up marriage, so asking didn't seem all that risky. I'd been attracted to you for a long time. Months. And I figured that you had to be at least a little interested if you were willing to marry me. Was I wrong?"

She lifted one shoulder in a half shrug.

"Let me ask that a different way. If Jeffrey had been in the same predicament . . ."

A smile tugged at her lips. "He'd have been out of luck."

That was all the confirmation I needed.

I dropped to one knee. "Ava, I'm horrible at dating. I lack confidence, and I second guess myself. But one thing I am good at is loving someone. And I love you. My feelings have nothing to do with anything I overheard in the kitchen. And I love you more now than the day I married you. All the promises I made that day to love, honor, and cherish . . . I meant every word."

She stared at the ground.

"I held back and didn't tell you that I love you because I didn't want you to feel pressured. Instead, you assumed I wasn't interested in that way."

She sucked in a deep breath.

"I am interested in that way. I want to be your safe place. I want you to trust me . . . with your heart. And the rest of you. I'm not your husband because I needed your help. I *want* to be married to you."

Her gaze snapped from my knee on the ground to my face. "You really don't like pie?"

"It's the crust. Sometimes the filling is okay, like lemon. I like that filling, but I don't like the doughy crust." Why was I on one knee talking about pie?

"Have you ever had it in a graham cracker crust?"

In that moment, I understood. She wasn't talking about pie because she wanted to avoid the conversation. Only because she was nervous.

"Ava, sweetheart, I'm not going to discuss pie with you right now. Or the weather."

She walked around the tree, then came back and stopped in front of me. "Say it again."

"I love you. Every inch of you . . . visible and hidden. I love the way you smile in the morning before you've had even a sip of coffee. I love how you go out of your way to help others no matter the cost to you. And I love the feel of your body pressed against mine. I find you incredibly attractive, but your beauty isn't just on the outside. You're beautiful inside and out."

Her smile disappeared, and her chin quivered.

With the chocolate melting in my hand, I just kept going. "I love you just the way you are and especially with your hair down."

"What if I cut it all off?" The corners of her mouth lifted into a small smile.

"I'll still love you." The rock under my knee was starting to hurt. But my grand gesture would seem less so if I had had to shift.

"You don't regret marrying me?"

"Not a bit. I only regret not being honest about my feelings sooner."

"I probably wouldn't have believed you." She sucked in a deep breath.

I tossed the chocolate on the ground and clasped her hands. "Ava, will you let me love you? I want to share my life with you and my bed." I wasn't holding anything back.

She stepped closer to me. "I—"

A door slammed, and I held my breath, hoping she'd finish her sentence before we were interrupted.

"Miss Ava, we found you!" Mason ran up beside me.

Parker ran up less than a second later. "Mason, buddy, let's go back to the truck."

"But we found her." Mason cocked his head and reached for Ava's hand. "Why are you crying?"

She wiped her face. "I'm okay."

I wasn't.

They'd crashed our little talk at the absolute worst time. And the look on Parker's face signaled that he'd figured that out.

Mason, however, had no clue. His eyes narrowed as he focused on me. "Did you make Miss Ava cry? I don't like it when she cries."

Honesty was the best policy, right? "I did, but I'm trying to fix it. I don't like it when she cries either."

Mason cupped a hand around my ear and whispered, "Maybe you should kiss her."

Funny thing, I was about to try that before he stomped up.

"I will later."

He looked at Ava and flashed a wide smile. "Don't cry. No one makes pies better than you do. You're the best."

Ava covered her face, and her shoulders bounced. I wasn't sure if she was laughing or crying.

Panic etched on Mason's face. "Did I make her cry?"

"Sometimes saying nice things makes her cry. But she's okay. I think."

Ava hugged Mason. "I'm okay. And thank you. I'm glad you like my pie."

Parker dragged his hands through his hair. "I'm so sorry." He tugged Mason back toward the truck.

I knocked the rock out from under my knee and stood because the moment was gone. Forever. "I thought there was no trail to here."

Ava inhaled a blew out a breath. "Not a good one, but the ranch hands come out here sometimes and do target shooting." She pointed at the target stuck to a tree, then at the tire tracks on the ground. "They just drive through the fields."

"You could've had one of the ranch hands drive you over today instead of lassoing a stump."

She laughed. "Bet you didn't know I could do that."

"Now I know not to run away from you when you're holding a rope."

"I didn't want any of the other guys to see me crying." She brushed the last few tears off her face. "They'd want to know what was wrong, and I didn't want them to blame you."

"I appreciate that. I think they'd be pretty unhappy with me."

I opened my arms, and she buried her face in my chest.

Mason waved. "Are you coming to the party?" He slapped a hand over his mouth, then looked up at Parker. "I ruined the surprise."

Parker patted Mason's head. "Doesn't matter." He opened the door of the truck and herded Mason inside. "I didn't mean to interrupt y'all, but I came to check out here because Kent said you were upset and had run off somewhere. Then Beau texted that he heard what sounded like a gunshot." He flashed a grin. "They weren't sure how much trouble you were in."

Ava's eyes widened. "I would never . . ."

"A bag of chips. I stepped on it." I'd probably never hear the end of this.

She looked back at the porch. "I knew I'd grabbed two bags."

Parker kicked at the dirt. "Should we go, or do y'all want a ride back?"

She touched a hand to my cheek. "We can talk later."

"Sounds good. Besides, they have a surprise party planned." I rubbed her back. "It's a pool party and not much of a surprise."

She pressed a kiss to my neck. "Then we should go get our swimsuits on."

"Yeah. But before we leave, I need to know you're okay."

She inched up on her toes and kissed me like we were back in the hallway covered in lemon goo. "Better than okay."

The truck door slammed, and I waved to let Parker know we were coming. I didn't want to have Ava lasso us across the river or crawl across using the ladder as a bridge. We'd lived dangerously enough for one day.

She picked up her snacks, then clasped my hand.

I wasn't really looking forward to the party. Spending time alone with Ava sounded much more appealing.

But for that—and whatever she was going to say—I'd have to wait.

CHAPTER 31

I climbed into the passenger seat of Mad Dog's truck. "We'll come back and get mine later. And I'm sorry I left without saying goodbye at church."

"Don't feel bad. I didn't tell anyone I was leaving either." He shrugged. "I'm guessing they've figured it out by now."

Thinking about him running out to find me without a second thought challenged so many of my assumptions. "We need to go back over there. People are probably still there. You can at least let Gary know you're okay and then say goodbye to the stragglers."

"Are you sure? If you'd rather not go, I understand."

I grabbed his hand. "I want to go. Mrs. Beecham is unkind, but I think it's because she's unhappy. I can be kind and show her what happiness looks like." Wiping my face, I prayed my eyes wouldn't look like I'd spent an hour crying.

Mad Dog shook his head. "I don't know how you do it. That's an amazing attitude, Ava."

My motives weren't completely pure. "Now that I know you love me, showing up with you is like rubbing her nose in it." I grinned. "That part isn't so amazing, huh?"

He laughed. "At least you're being honest."

"As long as I'm being honest . . ."

"Uh-oh. Should I pull over?" He shot me a side glance.

"No. Keep driving." I pinched the soft spot on my hand. "This whole time, I thought you were making the best of the situation. That you were just trying to be kind. I didn't think . . . you could feel that way about me." I didn't think anyone could feel that way about me.

"I wish you could see yourself through my eyes."

I wished the same thing, but since I couldn't, I'd just have to trust him. "You don't have to leave when I do my belly dancing classes."

He grinned. "I'm looking forward to that."

We parked in the church lot. There were still several cars in the lot. Not everyone had left.

He clasped my hand as we walked toward the building, and when he pulled open the door, he winked. That set my mind to wondering. What was he going to do?

We followed the voices, and when we stepped into the meeting room, people clapped.

Gary stepped up beside Mad Dog. "We wondered where you disappeared to."

"I had to run back to the ranch. Sorry I didn't say anything." Mad Dog kept a firm grip on my hand.

Gary motioned toward the snack table. "I hope you didn't want any pie. We finished them all off while we were waiting for you." He shrugged apologetically. "I might've eaten more than my fair share."

I smiled up at Mad Dog. "That's fine. I'll make him all the pie he wants."

My new goal in life was to find a pie that he liked. But that wasn't my only goal.

Mad Dog squeezed my hand. I thought he was acknowledging our inside joke, but when I heard Mrs. Beecham huff beside me, I knew the hand squeeze was a warning.

I smiled as I turned, reminding myself that her misery would follow her home. I, on the other hand, was going home with Mad Dog.

Before she had time to spew any of her opinions, Mr. Beecham tapped her on the shoulder. "Don't forget to ask Ava for that recipe. That's the best pecan pie I've ever tasted."

Her jaw clenched a second, then a forced smile spread across her face. "When you have time, I'd like to get that."

"I can write it out for you now. There is usually a notepad in the kitchen."

It had to be difficult for her to ask me for the recipe, so I didn't gloat. Visibly. Inside, I did a wicked little dance which included a lot of hip jiggling.

Mad Dog leaned in close and kissed my cheek. "I'm going to visit a bit while you write it out for her."

"I won't be long."

Mrs. Beecham eyed me as we walked into the kitchen and as I rummaged through a drawer to find a note pad and pen.

When I found what I needed, I scribbled out the recipe, bracing for whatever unhappy thing she felt the need to say.

"It won't last, you know." She raised her eyebrows.

"Very true. I'd eat it within four days, but it rarely lasts that long. The guys at the ranch devour them almost as soon as they come out of the oven."

My feigned ignorance clearly irritated her.

"I meant your marriage."

Those words would have destroyed me even a day ago because then I believed the same thing. Not anymore. "Not long ago, I might've agreed with you. But Mad Dog is too good to let him slip away. All marriages take work. But he's worth it."

Mrs. Beecham's mouth hung open, and she blinked.

Did I win an award for rendering her speechless? "What's your secret to having such a long and successful marriage?"

"He likes to eat." She snatched the recipe out of my hand and marched away, seemingly offended by my question.

So much for trying to be nice.

I made my way across the room to Mad Dog. He'd be tired of shaking hands after today. I could stand here and smile or I could clean up.

Tempting as it was to stay busy rather than feel like I was on display, I stayed next to him. The room cleared out pretty quickly once people had a chance to say goodbye. It wasn't as if he was leaving town. He just wasn't going to preach every Sunday.

Mad Dog slipped an arm around my waist. "Ava and I have plans, so we should head out." He stuck his hand out to Gary. "I'll be around if you need anything."

Gary smiled. "Dinner occasionally would be nice."

"We can do that." I needed to find the man a sweetheart.

Mad Dog was quiet as we drove back to the ranch. As much as I wanted to continue the conversation we'd started at the old cabin, I didn't want to have that conversation interrupted by the party.

I didn't want anything else interrupted by the party either.

When we arrived at the house, I leaned across the cab and kissed his cheek. "It won't take me long to change."

He nodded. "Great. I'll meet you back at the truck in just a few minutes."

"Perfect." I hurried into my room and closed the door.

Before digging out my swimsuit, I reached into the recesses of the drawer where items rarely—mostly never—saw the light of day. I pulled out the piece Lilith and Joji had left on my bed. After putting it on a hanger, I hung it on the closet door.

It was no longer a question of feeling loved or trusting him. It all came down to courage.

I'd have to see how brave I felt after the pool party.

CHAPTER 32

MAD DOG

*W*e'd been at the pool for almost half an hour, and Ava still had on her cotton coverup. She'd also stayed at least an arm's length away from me since we'd walked onto the back patio.

She was like a brain teaser puzzle, and I wasn't smart enough to figure her out. I was second guessing everything she said and did. That frustrated me. She was better than okay. I should embrace the positive in that statement and quit wondering if I'd be a permanent resident of the guest room.

"Fajitas will be ready in two minutes. Afterward, we'll bring out dessert!" Lilith motioned to the table. "All the fixin's are over here. Drinks are in the cooler."

"What's for dessert?" Parker asked from the pool.

Joji pulled on her coverup. "Lemon bars." She turned to face Ava. "Clint mentioned that you'd made some the other day, and I haven't been able to stop thinking about them since."

"Awesome!" Mason fist bumped Parker before swimming to the side. "I need to dry off so I can eat."

Ava stepped up beside me. "I did not have anything to do with the dessert choice."

Leaning close, I answered so that only she could hear. "I'm a little shocked Clint mentioned that you made lemon bars to anyone. I wonder what else he told Joji."

Pink spread across her face. "He might not ever set foot in our house again."

Our. Never had a tiny little word sounded more beautiful.

I kissed her cheek. "At least not without someone letting him in."

Her smile sent me back into puzzle thinking. "Oh, I might've found someone to clean and cook on the weekends. She is going to call me. I'm hoping Beau will let her live in one of the cabins. Two are empty, so I doubt he'll care."

"Does that mean you aren't going to ask Beau about moving me into one of them?" I poked her in the side.

She rolled her eyes. "What do you think?"

Why couldn't she just answer my question?

Lilith and Joji set serving dishes on the table. And the smell of fajitas beckoned everyone to the table.

Ava slipped her fingers into my hand. "Am I ever allowed to talk about pie?"

I tugged her closer to me. "Sure. When the weather's bad, and we're snuggled in bed in the middle of the day."

"That might've been possible with your old job, but not now. Work on the ranch doesn't care about the weather." She hadn't pushed back against the idea of being snuggled in bed, just about the possibility of that happening. After picking up paper plates, she handed me one.

"True, but I'll see what I can do." Spending a day snuggled in bed—or even half a day—held great appeal. I had to figure out how to make that happen.

Tables were set up around the patio, and soon every seat

was full. Ava sat on one side of me, and Mason sat on the other.

"Mr. Mad Dog, will you still come swim with me when you're a cowboy?"

"Sure. Even cowboys take time to swim."

Mason giggled. "But not with boots on."

I tousled his hair. "You always give such great advice."

"You mean like about kissing?"

All conversation at the tables stopped, and Ava rested a hand on my leg. She was worried about what he'd say next. Poor Kent was probably holding his breath. That dad had his hands full with such a smart and talkative kid.

"Kissing, swimming. You know about a lot of stuff." I made eye contact with Clint who feigned wiping his brow.

Mason kept everyone on their toes. "My dad teaches me lots of stuff. And I learn stuff at school. Only letters and numbers really. Mr. Garrett said he'd teach me how to find people. He's kind of like a spy."

"Private investigator," Ava said.

Garrett grinned from the end of the table. "I kind of like being called a spy."

Mason tapped my arm. "When I grow up, I want to be a cowboy."

"You know almost as much as I do already." I tried not to laugh at Garrett's dejected shrug.

Conversation started again, and food disappeared one taco at a time. As much as I wanted to be somewhere alone with Ava after our conversation at the cabin, this kind of community was rare and not to be taken for granted.

How could I have known that marrying Ava would come with so many extras?

After everyone had stuffed themselves and devoured lemon bars, the party moved back to the pool.

Ava had shed her coverup and was bobbing in the pool,

chatting with the other ladies. I, on the other hand, was impersonating a shark and chasing Mason around.

When Parker stepped in to be a shark, I dried off and flopped into a lounge chair. With my eyes closed, I soaked up the late-afternoon sun.

When I heard movement beside me, I opened my eyes. Ava draped her towel over the lounge chair beside me.

Instead of sitting down, she glanced at her cover-up and then at me.

Hoping I wasn't imagining the gleam in her eye, I smiled up at her. "Hello."

The way she looked at me sent excitement racing through my veins. Maybe she did want to be more than married roommates.

Pointing at my chair, she asked, "Mind if I sit here?" There was a hesitant edge to her voice.

I shifted and dropped a leg over each side, making room for her to sit in front of me. "Have a seat."

"Think it will hold both of us?" She started to step away.

I caught her hand. "I think it'll be fine. If it doesn't hold us, we'll find a different chair."

She eased down onto the seat. All day, worry that I'd waited too long to be honest about my feelings had nagged me. I wouldn't make that mistake again.

I rested my hands on her hips and gave them a quick squeeze. "Perfectly shaped for me to hold."

She pulled my arms around her and leaned back against my chest. "Do you mean me or my hips?"

"Yes."

Now I really wanted to go home.

Beau whistled. "If I could get everyone's attention. I know some people need to go, but before anyone leaves, I want Mad Dog to open his gift." He stepped inside and returned with a box wrapped in newspaper. "Lilith wasn't around, so I wrapped it. Can you tell?"

Lilith shook her head.

Clint stepped up beside Beau. "I think you were born for ranch work, but one thing really needs to change, so we all pitched in to get you this."

Ava started to get up, but I pulled her close as Beau walked over to hand me the gift.

I dropped a kiss on her shoulder. "You don't have to get up." I tore the paper off the box and laughed. "Are y'all trying to say you don't like my old hat?"

"Pretty much." Clint chuckled.

The ranch hands laughed.

Ava patted my leg. "Put it on. I want to see how it looks."

The new cowboy hat was a perfect fit. "Thanks, everyone."

Joji climbed out of the pool and walked over as she dried off. "I'm sorry we can't stay longer, but Nacha and Hank are coming over tonight."

Clint eased up beside her. "Good luck. You know we're around if you need anything." He checked the time and nudged Joji. "We don't want to be late. I want to put that new toy together before the baby gets to the house."

Joji rubbed his arm. "This guy spoils that little girl. But it's so fun. I swear he spends half the evening on the floor playing with her when they come over."

"Thanks for today. I appreciate it." I was glad we'd chosen to live here on the ranch and not next door to Mrs. Beecham.

Clint pointed at me. "You're part of the family. Like it or not." Laughing, he walked away.

Joji ran to catch up with him.

"I think I'm ready to go home." I whispered in Ava's ear before dropping a kiss on her neck.

She nodded.

~

SILENCE HUNG in the air on our drive home.

When I parked, Ava was out of the truck and in the house before I could say anything. That wasn't what I'd expected. And when I walked inside, she was already closed up in her room.

Maybe she really just meant that we'd talk later. Only talk.

I had other things in mind. After a quick shower, I pulled on a pair of jeans. "Ava, want a glass of wine?"

Her door opened a crack. "No thanks."

Wanting to know what she was thinking, I asked one more question. "Should I lock the door?"

I barely caught sight of her nod before the door closed again.

The woman had mastered the tease. And my guess was she hadn't intended to tease at all.

After locking the door, I stood at the end of the hall, trying to decide what to do.

Her door opened again, and she peeked around it. "Sorry I took so long. I was . . ." Chewing her lip, she looked at the ground a second then met my gaze again. "Do you want to . . .?" The end of the question dangled in the air . . . another tease.

I was done second guessing what I should or shouldn't say. "I want you."

"What you said out at the cabin . . . I don't think we should share your bed." She stepped out from behind the door and had the front of her robe gripped together in one hand.

I reached for her, hoping she'd change her mind. "Ava—"

She touched a finger to my lips, and the robe hung open,

giving me a glimpse of something pretty. "I think we should share mine."

I pulled her into my arms. "I've been waiting for this."

"Me too." She rested her forehead against my chest. "I'd be lying if I said I wasn't nervous. But because I love you I want to *love* you."

"I love you too. And we'll take things slow. Like molasses."

She gasped as I dropped kisses on her collarbone. "Molasses. Maybe you'd like a molasses pie if I made it with the right crust. I think some people call it Shoofly Pie."

I walked her backward a few steps, then kicked the door closed. "I'm sure I'll love it."

She trailed a finger on my chest, drawing a heart. "We can talk about pie later."

I slipped the robe off her shoulders. "Perfect."

CHAPTER 33

I handed Mad Dog a glass of wine then sat down and draped my bare legs across his lap. I hadn't worn a night shirt around him with the exception of the two nights he'd stayed in my room. And then I'd been buried under the covers. Most of the time.

But my fear of the unknown had been replaced by a delight with the known.

"What time do you have to be at the ranch tomorrow?"

He eyed me over the rim of his glass. "I start Monday. Maybe we should stay in bed tomorrow." His eyebrows danced.

"Maybe in the afternoon. But I don't think we should skip church on Gary's first Sunday."

"Are you really okay continuing to attend that church?" Between sips of wine, he dotted kisses on my face and neck.

I shifted to give him better access. "There is *one* person who isn't nice . . . maybe two or three. The rest are good and kind. I don't want to leave, but I've been thinking that volunteering in the kitchen isn't the best idea. I don't think I'll do that for a while."

"I support that decision one hundred percent." He ran his hand up my leg. The feel of his fingers on my skin was still new and exciting.

"I've been thinking about what you said when we were out by the cabin."

"Which part? I said a lot of things." He continued dropping kisses on my neck.

"About not having confidence and second guessing yourself. I wouldn't have thought that. And it surprises me. Did you just not notice that other ladies at church vied for your attention?"

His head snapped up, and a little crease appeared between his eyebrows. "What are you talking about?"

"You're a good catch." I leaned forward and sealed my lips to his, taking in every detail—the richness of the wine on his lips, the roughness of his fingers as they gently grazed my neck, and the soft moan of contentment. This was what happily ever after felt like.

When he broke away, he cradled my face. "I love you." His husky whisper sent shivers dancing down my spine.

"I didn't know it could be this way." I'd lied to myself for a long time and those lies kept me from seeing the truth.

"Marriage?"

"My life." Just as I leaned in again, a knock sounded at the door.

Mad Dog grinned. "Hold that thought. My order is here."

"Your order? No one delivers out here. When I order pizza, I have to send one of the guys to pick it up in town."

Laughing, he opened the front door and picked up a small cooler. "You just have to know who to call." He unzipped the top and lifted out a foiled covered plate. "I had a craving for lemon bars."

"Please tell me you didn't ask Clint to bring them over."

My vision of how that call went was both horrifying and hilarious.

He shook his head. "I didn't want to traumatize your brother. I messaged Beau and told him porch delivery was preferred. I promised to return the favor when he needed something."

"He'll be asking for a midnight pie in less than a week." I pushed off the couch. "I'll get plates."

Mad Dog pulled me against him. "Unless there is some kind of emergency, I'm the only one who will be asking for anything at midnight." His lips grazed mine. "We don't need plates."

"Crumbs will get everywhere." I couldn't have walked away from him if I'd wanted to. My legs refused to move. My body had practically melted to the couch.

He held out a lemon bar, wanting me to take a bite. "I'll clean them up."

Besides the tiny piece of cake at our wedding, I'd never been fed by someone else. But I liked it.

We snuggled together on the couch, feeding each other lemon bars and talking about the future.

It seemed surreal to be planning a vacation with my husband.

"I know the weather isn't bad and we aren't snuggled in bed, but I really need to talk to you about not liking pie. It seems . . ."

"Wrong?"

"Well, yeah. If you don't like the crust, I can make a different kind. I could try a graham cracker crust or a short-bread crust like what's used for the base of lemon bars. What about the insides of pies?" Completely aware of how absurd it was to be talking about pie when he was being so roman-tic, I couldn't help myself. How could anyone not like pie?

He kissed the side of my mouth. "You had a bit of lemon there." His trail of kisses continued across my mouth and down my neck. "You didn't have lemon in the other spots." His gaze swept over the rest of me. "Maybe I should check elsewhere."

"Is this you not wanting to talk about pie?"

He laughed. "We can talk about pie. I don't like squishy fruit. The inside of a pecan pie is fine, but on those I don't like the crust. I've never had a graham cracker crust. I love lemon bars, so if you can make a pie taste like that, I'm game to try it."

"Yay. I can't wait to make you a pie you like."

"Oh! Speaking of like . . ." He stood. "I'll be right back."

Half a minute later, he walked out of the guest room, carrying a box of Peeps. "I bought these for you."

"You remembered."

"Making you happy has been my priority since before I proposed. So, yeah. I remembered."

I tugged him back down next to me. "I know what we're doing tomorrow. We're roasting Peeps."

"In bed? That sounds dangerous."

"Who knew you'd be so funny?" I trailed a finger down his bare chest. "If you're feeling really adventurous, I can show you a spot in the river that's great for swimming and far away from other people." Even I was surprised by the words coming out of my mouth.

"I'm starting to like this ranch more and more." He reached over and bolted the front door. "Finish your wine, then we'll crawl in bed."

I drank down the last of my wine. "I hope you weren't planning to sleep in the guest room."

"But all my stuff is in there." Mischief danced as sparkles in his brown eyes.

I leaned in close to his ear. "I'll help you move everything into *our* room."

"I'd be crazy to turn down your help."

EPILOGUE

JEFFREY

Mad Dog hopped out as soon as I parked in front of the dilapidated cabin. "I'll be just a minute."

"You aren't intending to actually go in there, are you?" Usually, I was the one doing crazy things.

Rubbing the back of his neck, he stared at the cabin. "Only for a second. I wanted you here in case the whole place comes down on my head."

"So I can what? Call Ava and apologize that I didn't stop you from doing something royally stupid?"

He shook his head. "I'll try not to die. But if I do, tell her I wanted to surprise her with something memorable for Christmas."

"That's not funny." Standing beside the truck, I held my breath as he grabbed the porch rail and tested each stair on the way up.

Mad Dog peeked in the windows, then pushed open the front door. He stared inside.

"Wait!" There was no way I could let him go into that cabin.

He eased back off the porch. "What?"

"I'll go. Just tell me what I'm supposed to get." I laced my fingers, then stretched them, hearing every knuckle pop. "Seriously."

"No. I'm trying to figure out the safest way to get a bench out of there. I can see it from the doorway, but that floor looks pretty rotted." Mad Dog dragged his fingers through his hair. "I'm open to good ideas."

"Is that your subtle way of saying that me going inside is a bad idea?"

He smirked. "It's like you're a mind reader."

"Let me look." I moved up the steps, surprised at how little they creaked. The porch, however, groaned as I stepped on it. Peering through the front door, I could just make out the side of an old bench. "That bench isn't in great shape. Have you considered getting your wife something *nice* for Christmas?"

"It has sentimental value. But it's going to take some work to fix up. I plan to do that in your barn so that Ava won't accidentally see it."

After counting off the paces in my head from me to the bench, I scanned the ground around the cabin. "I have an idea. If it works, neither of us have to go inside."

"Great. Because I'd be happy if you didn't have to tell Ava that I'd been stupid."

"You and me both." I grabbed a shepherd's hook from the bed of my pickup. "Grab that long stick over there, will ya?"

Mad Dog dragged it over to the truck. "What's the plan?"

"I was planning to put lanterns up around the serving table at the shindig tonight. I'm also going to drape lights over the serving table. Holiday lights is the theme, right?" I lashed the hook to the stick with rope and tied it off tight. "Anyway, I think we can use this hook to catch the leg of that bench and drag it to the door."

"It's worth a shot."

"What time are we supposed to meet Lilith over there?"

He checked the time. "In less than an hour. But we aren't meeting Lilith. She and Beau left today for their second honeymoon. Ava is helping out."

"Lilith really just needs to hire someone to coordinate events." I used the hook to push the door open the rest of the way.

Mad Dog laughed. "Beau said the same thing, so she did. I haven't met her yet, but she started last week. Ava said she's nice."

Together, we maneuvered our makeshift tool toward the old bench. "Why is this thing important?"

"Ava loved this place, and Clint made that bench for her a long time ago. She said once that she regrets not getting it out before the cabin started to collapse."

With the hook in place around the leg of the bench, I motioned for Mad Dog to pull back slowly. "You mean Ava had the sense not to walk into this cabin?"

"Just pull the bench to the door, then I won't have to go in either."

As soon as the bench was within arm's length, Mad Dog picked it up. "I can't thank you enough."

"What are friends for besides keeping each other out of danger?"

"Let's drop this off in the barn, then head over to the venue. If we're late, Ava might ask why."

As soon as I pulled up to the venue, Mad Dog jumped out. "I'm off to find Ava. You know where to go."

I drove to where the table was always set up. Setting up the lights was the first item on my list. Poles were already in place at each end of the long table. All I needed was a ladder.

Scanning the area, I walked toward the main office to ask Ava. Mad Dog had joked about how she hid ladders. Would I have to beg to be able to use one?

But only a few paces from the eating area, I noticed a ladder leaning against a tree.

Perfect.

I carried it back to the table and climbed up to work on the lights.

"Hey! Bring that back." A voice echoed, but there was no person attached to the voice that I could see.

Inching backward down the ladder, I looked around. "Hello?"

"Put the ladder back. What part of that is hard to understand?" Somewhere close by there was a woman, and she wasn't happy with me.

I just couldn't see her.

That was kind of the story of my life—women who weren't happy with me. I strolled to the tree where I'd picked up the ladder. In the branches was the unhappy woman. She brushed blonde hair out of her face and stabbed at me with a determined blue gaze. "Are you trying to land me in the hospital?"

"Need help getting down? I can catch you." It had worked for Clint. Why not try his method?

She huffed. "No, I don't want you to *catch* me. I want you to put the ladder back."

"What are you doing up there?"

"Spacing the strands of lights." She sighed. "Will you please get the ladder?"

"Sorry, yeah. I didn't see you in the tree." I grabbed the ladder and put it back against the trunk. "You can come down now. I'll hold it while you do."

"Just back away. I got up here without anyone holding it. I should be fine getting down without help." Her tall, thin frame eased down the rungs.

When the ladder started to tip, I reached out. I'd be blamed for this. But I could live with that.

Wrapping my arms around her waist, I pulled her up against me as the ladder hit the ground. "Hello, I'm Jeffrey."

She shoved on my chest. "I know who you are."

Ava waved as she hurried toward us. "Oh good, I caught you both together. Jeffrey, this is Mindy. She's the new coordinator. You'll be working with her most of the time from now on."

"Fabulous." I'd managed to sour that relationship in record time. Working with Mindy would be fun. So much fun.

Ava looked at Mindy. "This is Jeffrey, the Cowboy Chef. He does a lot of the catering out here."

Mindy looked me over like I was a bull at an auction, one that wasn't expected to bring a good price. "Your reputation precedes you."

Crap. Pretty sure she wasn't referring to a restaurant review.

~

Keep reading for a Bonus Epilogue!

BONUS EPILOGUE

MAD DOG

I turned the page of my newspaper, pretending to read while Ava belly danced along with the rest of her online class. Making it home to watch wasn't always possible, but it was a treat when my schedule allowed me to be here.

Ava wiped her face as the class ended. "Let me shower, then I'm all yours."

"I have an idea."

She stopped at the end of the hall. "What's that?"

"Let's open our presents early. It's only two days until Christmas." I wasn't going to be able to keep the gift a secret much longer. And my reasons for giving her the other gift were completely selfish.

Shaking her head, she laughed. "You are like a grown-up kid. I'll grab yours out of its hiding place."

I pulled the sofa away from the wall and slipped out one gift. Then I ran out to the truck to get the other one. I'd grabbed it from Jeffrey's shed earlier today, and my patience wasn't going to hold out much longer.

Ava walked into the living room a few minutes later, her

wet hair pulled up into a knot. "I didn't even take time to dry my hair."

"Good. Because I really want you to open this." I patted the big box on the coffee table.

After setting a box on the end table, she sat down beside me. "That one is for you."

"Open this. Then I'll tell you a story."

She shot me one of those intoxicating side glances. "Am I going to like the story?"

"Just open it."

Once she had the box open, she stared inside. "Why did you risk going into that cabin?" Tears slipped down her cheeks. "It was too dangerous. You shouldn't have done that."

I lifted the bench out of the box. "I didn't go into the cabin. And you can thank Jeffrey for that."

Staring at the blue bench, she bit her bottom lip. "I love it. More than love it."

"Good. I hope you'll like the other gift too. I'm sure I will."

"Two gifts?"

"You'll understand when you open it." I handed her the other gift.

When she lifted the lacy bodysuit out of the box, her cheeks flushed. "You went to Delaney's shop, didn't you?"

"I did. She had a flyer in her window about setting up personal shopping times. So, I had help. Beau, Clint, and I went over there together." I watched as she fingered the snaps.

"Y'all went together?"

"There's strength in numbers, but I didn't pay attention to what the other guys bought. That would just be weird." I rested my hand on hers. "Do you like it?"

"I have a story to tell you."

If it weren't for her slight grin, I would've been concerned.

"Is that a yes? If you don't, we can return it. She said that wouldn't be a problem."

She ran a hand down my shirt. "I love it."

Ava told me about her past experience with a bodysuit, and with the animated way she recounted the story, I was almost in tears from laughing.

"I don't care if you never wear it outside the house. That wasn't why I bought it."

"Open yours." She set the box in front of me.

I tore the paper off. "A SansAmp!"

"For your bass. I had a little help from Beau and Clint. They said you'd like this."

"I love it. It's perfect."

She moved the gift to the table and shifted into my lap. "Madog, you are still the best gift of all."

Finding true love twice in a lifetime was a rare gift.

"I love you too."

I LOVED WORKING on Jeffrey's ranch, but at the end of the day, I was dead on my feet.

Ava was humming as I walked into the house. "Hi, sweetheart." She was in her leggings, swaying her hips to music playing on the radio.

"This is a treat. I thought you'd be at the mess hall." I was used to coming home to an empty house and showering before racing to the main house for dinner.

"Prepped everything early. And Goldie is handling the rest." She wiped her hands on her apron, the same one I'd given her the night of our first date. "I've been working on a surprise."

"Oh?"

Running a hand up my chest, she smiled. "Go shower. The meatloaf will be ready soon."

"Special occasion?"

She inched up and kissed me. "Go get cleaned up. I also made a lemon bar pie."

"You are definitely up to something."

Laughing, she walked back into the kitchen. "I picked up a few more bottles from the winery. And I met Jeffrey's sister. Why didn't you tell me she owned the winery?"

"It never came up." I trudged down the hall, wondering what grand scheme she was cooking up.

While I showered, I thought about what day it was. Was I forgetting an anniversary? She'd made all my favorites. It wasn't my birthday, and it wasn't hers either. I had multiple reminders set on the phone to remind me about that day.

When I walked back out to the kitchen, she handed me a glass of wine. "Have a seat."

"Is there something you want to talk about or ask me?" I'd enjoy dinner better if I had a clue about what was up.

She rubbed my back. "Yes. Let's get food, then we'll talk."

I heaped meatloaf and mashed potatoes onto my plate. And shoveled in a few bites before tapping on the table. "What's up?"

"A couple of things. Are you ready for your gig tomorrow?"

I couldn't believe I'd joined a band. My life had flipped upside down in the best of ways after marrying Ava. But from the outside, it probably looked like I was reveling in a mid-life crisis.

"Yes. The Stargazing Cowboys are ready to perform tomorrow afternoon." I sipped my wine. "I know you didn't make all my favorites just to ask me that."

"I'm excited. The last performance was great."

"You going to wear that shirt again?"

She lifted her eyebrows. "And look like a total groupie? Absolutely."

"Good. Tomorrow morning, I'm meeting up with the guys to practice our set." How long would I have to wait for her real question?

"I invited Verbena. She might come." Grinning, Ava didn't look up from her plate.

"I should mention it to Gary. If he knows you're baking pies to take, he'll show."

"Good idea." She set her fork down. "Would you be okay with us keeping Mason for the weekend? Next weekend, not tomorrow. I know you're preaching on Sunday, so I wanted to clear it with you."

"Sure. I'm fine with that."

The question surprised me. Where was Kent going? He'd never gone away for the weekend without Mason.

Cool fingers touched my hand. "The protective guard dog inside can stand down."

"What do you mean?"

"You're a dad, and sometimes it's more obvious than others." She winked.

I wasn't following her train of thought. "What does being a dad have to do with Ke—oh." The thought of him dating someone bothered me a little. More like a lot, but I had no right to be irritated. "I'm fine keeping Mason. Did Kent meet someone?"

"He and Parker are going to look at some horses." Ava gripped my hand. "I know you like Kent for Poppy."

"As much as I like Kent, with Poppy in New York, I can't imagine how that would even work."

"But you tried to imagine how it could?" She kissed my fingers. "Finish eating."

"I want them both to be happy. Mason too."

"And now for the last question."

This one was going to be the doozy.

Ava sucked in a deep breath. "What would you think of visiting Ireland, Scotland, and Wales? I bet people over there will pronounce your name correctly."

I grabbed her hand. "That sounds amazing. After dessert, we can sit down with the calendar and figure out when we can steal away."

"Perfect." She stayed quiet while we finished our dinner. "Ready for pie?"

"Sure."

She called it pie, but it tasted exactly like lemon bars.

"Give me two minutes, then I'll get it." She disappeared down the hall.

After walking back into the kitchen, she set dessert on the table. "Let me grab the server."

She'd swapped her leggings for a robe.

I grabbed her hand. "You changed."

Twinkles danced in her eyes. "I went into town today. Joji and I stopped at Delaney's shop."

"Did you find something nice?" I had a feeling that if I got a peek under that robe, I'd know the answer to that question.

Grinning, she nodded. "Oh yeah. I think you're really going to like it, Madog."

I pulled her into my lap. "Pie can wait."

"I thought you'd say that." She kissed me, then hopped out of my lap. "Lock the door on the way to the bedroom."

"Yes, ma'am. Need help getting that robe off?"

In our marriage, we made helping each other a priority.

WANT to find out what happens with Mindy and Jeffrey? *Inspired by Mindy* is next in the series!

A NOTE TO READERS

Thank you for reading!

Ava first appeared in *Wrangled by Lilith*, and I knew she'd get her own story. But I wasn't sure who her love interest would be until writing Joji's story.

Mad Dog walked onto the page in the last part of *Two Words I'd Never Say Again*. And I couldn't stop thinking about the pastor with the funny nickname.

I love this story for lots of reasons. If you loved it, please consider leaving a review.

Be sure to check out my website for updates about the series and for information about my other books.

www.RemiCarrington.com

ABOUT THE AUTHOR

Remi Carrington is a figment of Pamela Humphrey's imagination. She loves romance & chocolate, enjoys disappearing into a delicious book, and considers people-watching a sport. She was born in the pages of the novel *Just You* and then grew into an alter ego.

She writes sweet romance and romantic comedies set in Texas. Her books are part of the Phrey Press imprint.

facebook.com/remiromance
twitter.com/phreypress
instagram.com/phreypress

Printed in Great Britain
by Amazon

30037579R00153